CRESCENT ROGUE

THE CRESCENT WITCH CHRONICLES - PREQUEL

NICOLE R. TAYLOR

CHAPTER 1

I was running.

Placing one paw in front of the other, I hurdled over fallen logs, wove through russet-colored ferns, and dodged trickling streams. I was lightning across the landscape, darkness nipping at my heels. Wolves were leaping behind me, saliva flying from their snapping jaws as they gained on my sleek form.

Red fur flew as jagged teeth crunched around my hind leg, and I yelped, twisting and rolling. Forcing the will to escape through my body, my bones snapped, and my fur began to grow.

Then I was flying, my wings beating faster and faster until I broke through the forest canopy and into the night sky, leaving the wolves behind on the ground below. Before long, black shadows broke away from the darkness above and fell, darting past my beak and buffeting my small body.

Danger! It permeated every sense, and I knew they would kill me if I were caught.

I dove, spiraling and zigzagging across the sky, the shadows bubbling and bulging until they formed the shape of a hundred inky ravens. As they whipped past me, their beaks and claws tore at my fragile wings, pulling feathers free and drawing blood. A shrill peal of alarm pierced the air, my beak opening and snapping at my attackers.

They buffeted me from side to side, swarming and smothering until I closed my wings and dove. My neck extended, my body straightened, and I broke through the trees and collided with a branch. There was a shower of leaves as I tumbled, slamming into another bough, and then another before slamming onto the forest floor. I rolled, my bones snapping and changing, stars bursting through my vision and fire tearing through my body.

The world spun, tumbling over and over, and then I was flat on my face, coming to an ungraceful stop in a clearing. Covering my face with my arms, a strangled moan tore from my lips, but the ravens didn't come. Peering at the sky, it was clear. The only thing that bore witness to the abrupt end to my flight was the thousands of stars twinkling down on me.

My hands curled through the undergrowth, dirt lodging under broken fingernails and leaf litter scratching against my palms. I was a man again, but how I knew was a mystery. The first thing I remembered was the four red paws of a fox and the white, speckled wings of a gyrfalcon. I was all three of those things, but I couldn't remember why.

Ahead, I heard the constant sound of crashing water. It was falling from a great height, slamming into a pool below, and the hiss of the wet spray showering on the rocks was barely audible above the din. Beside me was the snarled trunk of an ancient hawthorn tree, its branches bowing over the edge of the clearing like an umbrella.

When I rolled over, everything hurt. From the tips of my toes to the very hair on my head, there was pain. Moaning, I was aware I was completely naked, my skin bare to the sky above...and I was bleeding from what felt like a thousand cuts. The ravens had almost torn me limb from limb, but why?

Why?

Rustling drew my attention to the edge of the clearing, and my head snapped up. I almost expected the wolf pack to step from the darkness, their silver eyes glowing, their jaws snapping and thirsting for the kill, but it wasn't the wolves at all.

It was a woman. She was tall and slender, and her black hair was flecked with strands of silver. As she stepped into the moonlight, the air seemed to shimmer around her.

"*Fanacht amach*," I said with a raspy voice, attempting to drag myself toward the hawthorn tree. It felt safe there, the branches beckoning me under their canopy. "*Fanacht amach.*" *Stay Away.*

"Are you all right?" the woman asked, taking another step closer.

"*Cé hé mise?*" I asked, my voice sounding strange to my ears. "*Cé hé mise?*" *Who am I?*

I curled up against the trunk of the hawthorn, shielding my nakedness from the strange woman. I beat my fists against my head, my memory full of darkness and pain. "*Cé hé mise?*"

"Irish," the woman murmured to herself. To me, she asked, "Can you understand English? *An bhfuil Béarla agat?*"

Fisting my hands into my hair, I nodded. "Yes."

"What's your name?"

"Di..." I began, my tongue thickening in my mouth. No, that wasn't right. "*Di...*" I tried again, but my mind filled with noise. "I don't know."

She smiled softly. "I'm Aileen," she said. "It seems you've forgotten some things."

I cowered against the tree as she edged closer, fearful this was another trick. The sky was full of shadows that had turned into ravens. Maybe the woman would raise her hand and finish what had begun with the wolves.

"I saw you fall," she said, kneeling, her eyes never leaving me.

"I'm a man," I muttered. "A bird... A fox..."

"You're a shapeshifter."

"A what?"

"A man who can change his shape into any animal of his choosing...provided he's had contact with them," she explained. "I saw a gyrfalcon fall from the sky, tumble through the forest, and then land in this very clearing as a man. There's only one explanation for that."

A shapeshifter. That was what I was. A fox, a gyrfalcon, and a man.

"Whatever was chasing you, they've gone now." She pointed to the hawthorn. "The tree protected you."

"The tree?" I glanced up, wincing as pain flared down my spine.

"It's a hawthorn," Aileen explained. "The sacred trees of the fae and the witches. There's ancient power in her bones."

She spoke of the tree as if it were alive, and I placed my palm against the exposed root beside me. I could feel something—warmth—but I wasn't sure what it was. Honestly, I wasn't sure of anything. Even my own name eluded me.

"Where am I?"

"You're in the forest near the village of Derrydun," she replied, pointing to the north. "In County Sligo." I raised my eyebrows, not understanding, so she added another location. "Ireland."

"Ireland?" A thought flashed in my mind, and I knew wolves didn't belong here. There were no wolves in Ireland. Were they shapeshifters, too?

"You have the accent," she mused. "A very thick one...and know the language."

"There are no wolves in Ireland," I muttered.

Aileen frowned. "No, they were hunted down to the last almost three hundred years ago." Her gaze fell from mine and took in my shivering body. "You're bleeding quite badly, you know. You must be in a great deal of pain."

I tightened my grip on my hair. Every time I tried to remember what came before the running, a throbbing headache overcame me.

"So?" The woman shifted, pushing her weight back onto her heels. "Will you let me help you?"

I thought over my options. I was naked, wounded, likely had some broken bones, and I had no memory of who or what I was. My stomach was empty, I was lost, and I had no idea who to trust. Someone was looking for me, and they weren't nice at all. The wolves were trying to tear me apart, and the ravens would've shredded my flesh if they'd caught me. What could I do? I had nowhere else to go.

"I won't hurt you," Aileen said, her voice gentle. It had an almost musical quality to it, and as the notes fell over my body, warmth seeped into my bones. "I will keep you safe and clean you up. Derrydun isn't far, and it's protected by the hawthorn in the village green."

"Why?" I asked, my throat feeling completely raw.

Aileen smiled and laughed softly, the sound tinkling like sunshine through the darkness. "I would be a terrible witch if I turned away a creature of magic from my doorstep. Especially when he is in desperate need of a little help."

"A witch?"

"Aye, but I'm not just any witch." She smiled once more and rose to her feet. Holding out her hand, she beckoned. "I'm a Crescent Witch."

CHAPTER 2

The village was in darkness when we approached.

Aileen had graciously handed me her cardigan so I could maintain some sort of modesty on the short walk to her cottage. The pale blue fabric was tied around my waist, my bare backside shining for all eyes to see.

Limping through the forest, I'd made the going slower than it needed to be as rocks and prickles poked into my feet, not to mention the aches and pains that racked my body.

My left arm was tender to the touch, so I cradled it against my chest, assuming my wrist was either sprained or my forearm was broken. My back and sides stung from the cuts the ravens had inflicted in their swarming, and my right ankle felt bruised.

As we walked, I was sure Aileen had used her

magic when she'd spoken to me in the clearing, but she didn't use it again. I wondered why.

The further we ventured, the more understanding of the world poured into my confused mind. I knew witches cast spells and protected the earth, and I knew they had covens. Where there was one witch, there were many. I wondered where the others were. What had she said her coven was called? The Crescent Witches?

"Where are the other witches?" I asked.

"Not here," she replied, placing her finger over her lips. "We'll be home soon." Touching her ear, I understood she believed there were other ears in the forest. Remembering the chase, I fell silent. If the ravens appeared, I wasn't sure I would be able to thwart them again.

We climbed over a drystone wall and traversed a field, a sleepy flock of sheep peering at us as we passed. On the hill to our right, I saw the outer shell of an ancient tower glowing in the moonlight, the building crumbling into ruin and overtaken by nature. Then we clambered over another stone fence before moving into a manicured garden. The plants here were well tended, the flowerbeds immaculate and free of weeds.

The little cottage sat among the greenery, the little plot lush with flowers, herbs, and all sorts of shrubbery. A thatched roof sat atop two stories of whitewashed limestone walls, and one side of the house was covered in a thick layer of vines laden with red leaves—Virginia creeper. Beyond the garden, I could see more buildings and the glow of orange and white lights.

"That's Derrydun over yonder," Aileen said. "Not a hundred paces behind the cottage is my shop. It faces out onto the main road. There isn't much here, and few call this place home, but it's as good a place as any."

Mystified, I followed her up the garden path and to the front stoop where she fished a set of keys out of her pocket. Unlocking the door, she pushed it inward.

"In you go," she said. "Last thing anyone wants to see is your bare ass. One full moon is enough in these parts."

Stepping into the cottage, my nose filled with the earthy scent of herbs and the spice of cooking. The kitchen must be to the right, and further inside, I caught the whiff of flowery perfume and jasmine incense. My nose was sensitive, and I was amazed at my ability to pick out each thread from the cacophony surrounding me. It must be from the fox.

"Come in here," Aileen said, guiding me from the hall and into the kitchen.

She turned on the light, and the little space was illuminated. Within, there was a round table with four chairs, a refrigerator, and inbuilt cupboards. A stove and a large sink took up more space, and the benches were littered with pots, pans, and bowls of fresh fruit and vegetables. Inhaling, I was greeted with the scent of home. There were no threats here.

Pulling out a chair from the table, Aileen beckoned me to sit. I all but fell into the seat, collapsing into a heap with my back hunched.

She disappeared for a moment and returned with a blanket in her arms. In the light, I could see her more clearly than I had in the forest. Aileen was an older woman, perhaps old enough to be someone's mother, but she was far from being past her prime. The strands of silver running through her hair were a clue to her age, but I didn't want to ask.

"May I check your wounds?" she asked.

I nodded, and she pulled another chair close to mine and perched gingerly. The moment her fingers touched my skin, I flinched, jerking away and almost falling to the floor.

"*Shh*," she crooned like a mother who was calming her frightened child. "You've had quite the scrap. Does your wrist hurt? May I see?"

Another human's touch was unfamiliar and her kindness an alien concept after what I'd just been through, but I held out my left arm. This time, I didn't pull back when she cradled my wrist in her palm. Then as she inspected it, I could feel warmth again. *Magic.*

"It's healing quite nicely already," she said approvingly. "Very good, that."

"Why?"

"It's part of who you are. You have magic within, you know. It helps mend your bones when you change and when you break them. Even the scrapes on your back will heal over soon."

"Magic?" I repeated.

"Magic," she reiterated. "You're a very special young man. Your wounds will be righted in no time, of that I have no doubt."

Magic. She had it too, but we were different. Witch. Shapeshifter.

"You should wash," she went on, "but you look like you're half-starved. What a conundrum. Which shall we tend to first? Your stench or your belly?" My stomach growled, and she laughed. "Well, that settles it."

She draped the blanket around my shoulders, paying no mind to the state of her cardigan when I offered it to her. Opening the fridge, she took out a container and emptied some of its contents into a bright green bowl. Transferring the green dish into the microwave, she pressed in some numbers, and then the bowl began to rotate.

As I watched it spin, the hum droning in the

background, I wondered at my condition. I understood the world to a certain degree, but anything more complicated was beyond me. The harder I tried to make sense of it all, the more my head ached. Who I was and where I'd come from were the only things I wanted to know, but the answers were hidden behind a wall of pain.

The microwave beeped, and Aileen retrieved the steaming bowl, placing it on the table in front of me. Dropping in a spoon, she declared, "Traditional Irish stew. Homemade with vegetables from my very own garden. That'll put the hair back on your chest."

It smelled amazing, and I fisted my hand around the spoon and began greedily shoveling stew into my mouth.

She watched me eat with a raised eyebrow. "My, you are hungry. How many times did you change?"

I hesitated, the spoon pausing halfway between the bowl and my mouth. Taking a breath, I slowed my pace. It seemed some of the animals I'd changed into were lingering in my human form. Either that or the effort of shape-shifting made me ravenous. I wondered if the animal senses would fade away, at least until the next time I changed. *If I changed at all.*

"If I don't change, will I forget how?" I asked suddenly.

"I couldn't say," Aileen replied.

I glanced around the kitchen. "Where are the other witches? Your coven?"

"I'm one of the last," she explained. "Like the wolves, we've been hunted to the brink of extinction."

"Why would anyone want to harm you?" She seemed so nice and welcoming, I couldn't understand why.

She laughed. "I would like to know the same thing. I'm not quite sure why my crystals and tarot cards are offensive, but it seems someone really dislikes rose quartz."

"Why are witches being hunted?" I asked again, my brow creasing.

"That's a story for another time." She picked up the empty bowl and put it in the sink.

"Someone was chasing me," I said.

"I saw."

"I don't know why."

She didn't reply at first. Turning, she studied me, likely trying to determine if I was being truthful or not.

"Well, as long as you're in Derrydun, you'll be safe," she finally declared.

"Because of the hawthorn?" I asked, not entirely understanding why a tree was so important.

"That's right."

"I don't remember anything," I said, clutching

the blanket around my shoulders. "Just...running. And flying."

Aileen studied me, her eyes giving nothing away. "Never you mind. Things will sort themselves out. They always do when magic is involved."

"What do I do now?"

"We'll have a crack at it in the morning," she replied. "No use trying to figure out those kinds of things right now. You should rest up before any of that. When I think about it, you've just started living, like a babe who's just been born, or so says your foggy memory. You're asking question upon question like a wide-eyed five-year-old."

"I can stay?"

"Of course, you can."

I frowned, my full belly beginning to make me feel sleepy. The aches and pains I'd felt when I landed in the clearing were subsiding, and I wondered if Aileen was right. Maybe healing myself really was part of the magic she said I had. If that was true, then it was a welcome ability.

"If you're going to stay, then we have to call you something," she mused. "Do you have any ideas?"

I lowered my gaze, searching the kitchen for a clue. A name... She was Aileen, and I was... Staring at the newspaper on the table, I read the words printed on the front page.

"Boone," I said, saying one I liked aloud.

Aileen glanced at the newspaper, then back to me. "Aye, it does suit you, and it's normal enough. Boone you are, then."

"Boone," I said again, testing the sound of my new name.

"Now how about that shower?"

Aileen showed me to the bathroom and let me be, giving me my first taste of being alone since waking up in the forest.

Turning on the taps, I allowed the water to run, waiting while it heated. There'd been a waterfall near the hawthorn tree, but I hadn't seen it. The sound filling the bathroom reminded me of it, and flashes of my wild flight filtered into my mind's eye. The wolves and the ravens made of shadow. They were all things I remembered now. New memories.

Who was I? I didn't even know what I looked like. I didn't have any idea what color my hair or eyes were or if I was ugly or handsome. It was a mystery to me if I bore some of the physical similarities of the animals I'd changed into. Perhaps I had the eyes of a gyrfalcon and the pointed ears of a fox.

Steam filled the room, and I turned. Wiping my hand over the mirror to clear the fog, I studied my reflection with wide-eyed fascination. So that was what I looked like. It hadn't occurred to me to wonder at my appearance before now, but now I was staring at myself, I was perplexed.

Brown, almost black eyes peered back at me, and I had a strong brow with a sharp jaw that was coated with the shadow of thick stubble. I'd been clean-shaven once, but now the beginnings of a beard were growing. And to top it all off, a mop of disheveled black hair curled on my head, leaves and twigs sticking out of it. I was a mess, but I suppose I wasn't ugly.

I wiped the condensation off the mirror once more and committed my reflection to memory.

Boone.

CHAPTER 3

When I woke, it was day.

I'd become accustomed to the darkness, and now that light streamed in through the window, everything had changed. Again.

Aileen's spare bedroom was furnished with a mismatched set of colors and styles, the small space crammed full of items that didn't seem to have a place anywhere else. The framed tapestry of a fox and hound on the wall stared down at me, a mocking reminder of what I'd been when I woke the night before.

Easing out of bed, I sat on the edge and inspected my back, twisting my head in an attempt to see if the scratches left behind by the ravens had healed. They had, just like Aileen said they would.

Thinking about the witch, I wondered where she was. The cottage was silent. The only sound reaching my ears was the rustling leaves outside in the garden, stirred up by the breeze. Staring down at my nakedness, I tried to think of a solution for my predicament.

Looking around the room, I found a pile of clothes on the chair with a note on top. *Come to my shop, Irish Moon, when you're feeling up to it. - Aileen.*

Casting the paper aside, I sorted through the clothes. There were two pairs of trousers, two black T-shirts, a red tartan shirt, a thick slate gray knit sweater, a black coat, socks, underwear, and a pair of black boots that were creased around the toes and ankles. Placing the sole against my foot, they looked to be the right size. Aileen had thought of everything.

I helped myself to another shower to wash the sleep from my body and then dressed. The trousers were a little loose, but they would do. It was better than flashing my bare ass to the entire village, and it was a sight warmer.

Venturing into the garden, I shielded my eyes against the sun. It was overcast, the clouds breaking for a fraction of a minute and allowing warmth to seep into the earth below. My nose twitched, picking up the scent of soil, mint, and thyme from the pot beside the door, and beyond, the tang of lavender from the shrubs that bordered the path.

Glancing at the sky, I searched fruitlessly for the

ravens. There were no shadows here, and the longer I listened, the more I realized there was nothing malicious lingering among the rose bushes other than the thorns coating their stems. Derrydun seemed to be in its own little pocket of safety, blissfully unaware of the things that chased clueless foxes and flew after lone gyrfalcons.

Counting a hundred paces from the cottage to the street, I lingered at the corner, watching in fascination as a shiny red vehicle flashed by on the narrow stretch of road. A car driven by someone who barely got their license by the looks of it. It disappeared around the bend, and the village returned to its sleepy disposition once more.

Looking for Aileen's shop, I turned and found I was standing right next to it. A wrought iron fixture was screwed into the limestone, and a pale purple sign hung from the black metal that read Irish Moon. There was a crescent moon painted behind the lettering, and I remembered Aileen had said her coven was called the Crescent Witches. Maybe it was a nod to them or a calling card to others like her.

Opening the door, I stepped inside, a bell ringing above my head. The shop was small, but it was crammed full of books, trinkets, jewelry, and crystals. Lots of them. Geodes, slices, points, wands, caves, and stones covered every available surface and glittered in every color of the rainbow.

A calm and happy sensation washed over me, and I felt my shoulders lighten. Glancing at Aileen, who was sitting behind the counter, I tilted my head to the side, asking a silent question.

The witch nodded. "Aye, that's the crystals you're feeling. Nice, isn't it?"

"Very."

"And how are your aches and pains? Better, I presume?"

I nodded. "Thank you for the clothes."

"You're welcome. I got them from the lads down on the farm. Roy and Sean. I had to guess your size." She raised her eyebrow when I didn't reply. "Now if anyone asks, you're the son of a dear friend of mine, and you're staying with me. What we are is a secret, you see, and it must remain so. The human world mustn't know about our abilities. It's not that I like keeping the truth from them, but it's a perilous world we live in. To think a crazy woman with a shop full of crystals could cause mass hysteria is bonkers, but light a candle with your mind in front of the wrong person, and the world could implode. Next thing you know, they'll have me on an operating table trying to figure out what makes me tick. And you..." She shook her head and snorted.

"I understand."

"Do you?" She looked at me sternly, and my hackles rose.

"Perfectly." The last thing I wanted was to be chopped up and studied, not after my entrance into the world.

I glanced at the deck of oversized cards in Aileen's hands as she began shuffling them. They were all black with golden drawings, the metallic sheen flashing as they moved back and forth.

"Nice, aren't they?" she said, holding up the deck. "Tarot cards, they are. I got this set on Etsy."

I had no idea what an Etsy was, so I shrugged, my attention turning to the tubs of polished crystals on the shelf below the counter. Each had a label printed with the type of stone and what elements its power reigned over. Things like creativity, strength, and protection. I could feel the aura of the minerals through the entire shop, but I wasn't sure they worked that way.

"Come and sit," Aileen said, patting the empty chair beside her. "Would you like to draw a card?"

"What are they for?"

"Lots of things," she replied with a smile, shuffling the cards again. "Divination, advice, guidance. Sometimes, we're on a set path into our future and need a little reassurance...or a warning."

"You can see the future?" I asked, watching the cards.

"No one can see the future, at least, not any that's set in stone." Setting the cards on the countertop, she placed her palm on the top and swept it to the side, the cards fanning out in a long line. "Pick one."

I glanced at the cards, then at her.

"They aren't going to bite, you know," the witch said with a huff. "Pick one, and we'll see what it says. Perhaps it may give us a clue."

Standing opposite her with the counter between us, I reached out and allowed my fingers to brush over the cards. I assumed I could pick any I liked, and it wouldn't matter which if what she said was true. The card would pick me in the end and deliver a lesson I needed.

Drawing a single card, I turned it over and placed it face up on the counter.

There was a picture of a man lying facedown with swords stabbed into his back, and at the top was the Roman numeral for ten. All I could see was pain and loss, the thought of so many wounds on the man's back bringing to mind the torn flesh that had been on mine only the night before.

"Ten of Swords," she said, a hint of curiosity in her voice.

"What does it mean?"

"Every new beginning must come from an end, and with each defeat, a new future is born." She shook her head and peered at the card. "Curious."

I resisted the urge to scowl. Obviously, her

assessment could be applied to a shapeshifter with a memory spanning less than twelve hours.

She ignored me and continued, "The Ten of Swords usually means a sudden and unexpected failure, and is usually wielded by a power beyond your control. A power that has no mercy or feeling. In effect, something that completely blindsides you."

I grunted. It didn't mean much without knowing where I'd come from or who was hunting me.

"It can also indicate that you've been betrayed by someone you thought you could trust," Aileen went on, explaining the various interpretations. "But it's not a negative card, you know. There's hope after this challenge, and the sun will rise again. It's the darkest before the dawn and all that. The Ten of Swords is about letting go, accepting your current circumstances, and learning from defeat."

"How can I learn from something I don't remember?" I asked sullenly.

Before Aileen could reply, the shop door burst open, and a girl strode in. Earphones were stuck in her ears, the cord trailing down her chest and disappearing into her coat pocket. Her face was hidden behind a long stream of blue-black hair, and the big black boots on her feet thudded across the hardwood floors. The little bell above the door rang furiously in her wake, and she didn't once look up.

"Mairead, this is Boone."

The moment the girl's gaze met mine, her pale cheeks flushed red. She couldn't be a day over seventeen under all the makeup on her face. Her eyes were heavy with black coloring, and her lips matched.

"Mairead's a gothic," Aileen explained.

The girl rolled her eyes and pulled out her earphones. "Goth, Aileen," she declared in a heavy Irish accent. "*Goth.*"

Aileen smiled, and ignoring the correction from Mairead, she turned to me. "Boone is staying with me for a little while. His mother is a dear old friend of mine. Isn't that right?"

"Sure," I said hesitantly.

"I'm going to take him out into the village for lunch. You'll be fine here on your own, Mairead?"

Glancing at the girl, I blinked as her cheeks flushed deeper, and she turned away to avoid my gaze.

"Yeah," she replied. "I'll be fine."

The witch scooped up her tarot cards and placed them under the counter. Then she ushered me toward the door. "I shan't be long. Don't forget to dust!" she called over her shoulder.

Outside, Aileen started to laugh. "It's not fair of me to find it so amusing, but that girl pretends she hates everything, and one look at you and she's in love."

"I must be twice her age," I complained, looking up and down the street. A car *whooshed* by, fluttering her hair, and she smiled.

"I wonder how old you are," she mused. "I would say about twenty-five to thirty, but it's just a guess."

"Can you use magic to find out?"

"No, it doesn't work like that, and I shall not be using any of that nonsense away from the hawthorn in the forest."

"How does it work?"

"You and your questions," she said with a huff. "I can't tell you out here. You aren't the only creature that's hunted in these parts."

Frowning, I turned and looked at the village, thoroughly frustrated with the lack of answers the day had so far produced. There wasn't much to see, but Aileen proceeded to tell me all about it nonetheless.

"Welcome to Derrydun," she proclaimed. "Or *Doire Dún* in Irish. We have an assortment of curious folk here as well as their misshapen little establishments. Over there, we have Molly McCreedy's, the local pub."

I followed her pointing finger and studied the little limestone building with a thatched roof just like Aileen's cottage. It was almost overtaken by more of the Virginia creeper that seemed to be a fixture as much as the townsfolk were.

"There's a Centra supermarket and service station up yonder, just past the single set of traffic lights that no one ever pays attention to. See the building there with the lavender outside? That's Mary's Teahouse. She's a sweet little lady, who no one can ever understand—she speaks in Irish mostly and has a very thick accent—but she serves the best scones with clotted cream you'll ever have in your life. Derrydun is a popular stop on the tourist trail, so that's why you see all these gift stores."

"Tourist trail?" I asked, raising an eyebrow.

"We get busloads of tourists—travelers—who stop almost every day from March to October every year. It's how little places like this survive in the modern world. We sell our local legends, flavor, crafts, and produce to people from faraway places who've come to see Ireland."

We walked down the street side by side while I studied everything we passed. With every step, a growing need to solve the mystery of my past began to rise, like I knew it would. Shouldn't I know my identity? If I didn't know who I was, then how could I read the message from the tarot card? If this was a new beginning, then why did I have to lose my memory to get it?

There was something strange about Derrydun. The more I saw, the more I understood this was where I'd been running. I stared into the windows of shops, inhaled the scent of barley and hops from Molly McCreedy's, and when I saw the hawthorn in the middle of the road, I paused.

"Is that supposed to be there?" I asked, pointing to the tree imprisoned by a sea of asphalt.

"A hawthorn is always precisely where it's supposed to be," Aileen declared. "They're sacred in Ireland. Nobody will harm them, so as you can see, they built the road around it."

"This is the hawthorn that protects Derrydun?"

"The one and the same."

"Are we safe here?" I glanced at her nervously. "You say you're hunted, and you've been terribly kind..."

"I would not have invited you into my home if I thought you were a threat, Boone," she replied, weaving her arm through mine. "If something wants you, it's not a stretch to think it's the same something that wants to suck up all my magic."

"What—"

"I think that's enough of that," she interrupted. "We'll talk more at the cottage once the sun has set. For now, I think you should sample some of Mary Donnelley's scones and sandwiches."

I didn't have a choice in the matter as she hauled me across the street and into the teahouse. Of all the places I could've landed, it seemed Derrydun and its ancient hawthorn may have been my intended target after all. There was a witch who knew what I was and how my abilities worked and a deep magic that appeared to protect the whole area.

If there was any chance of recovering my memories and learning why I'd been pursued, then Aileen and this place may be the only lead I had. Maybe staying here would be a good idea.

Like I had a choice.

CHAPTER 4

The entire population of Derrydun seemed to be enthralled by my arrival. Lunch at the Teahouse was a spectacle with face after face looking in to see who the 'tall, dark, and handsome' stranger was.

Thrust into yet another unknown world, I retreated to Aileen's cottage and lingered in the garden, listening to the sounds of the village and the forest beyond. Staring up at the ruined tower house, I committed the rise and fall of the ruin to memory. I had no others to think on, so making new ones seem like a good idea. There was no use dwelling on a past that may as well have never been.

Nature seemed familiar and comforting as if my affinity with the animals I'd changed into had brought me closer to it. It was nice to feel a sense of belonging, so I sat in the garden, just...*existing*.

Aileen returned from her shop after the sun had dipped low in the sky, the first hints of twilight twinkling above.

"I promised you answers," she said, crooking her finger at me. "But I'm not sitting in the dirt. No way."

Standing, I brushed off my trousers and followed her inside. At first, she busied herself in the kitchen, chopping vegetables and filling a pot with water in which she placed meat and the squares of carrots, leeks, and potatoes she'd carved. Then the tangy scent of herbs filled the little room as she twisted various stalks and leaves in her hands before adding them to the pot as well.

I watched from my place on one of the kitchen chairs, itching to ask her a million and one questions.

"As you can see, stew is my specialty," she declared. "The secret is in the herbs. The fresher, the better. Can't get more Irish than that!"

"What—"

"After dinner," she interrupted. She was already feeling like a surrogate mother, and I grimaced. "There'll be plenty of time to ask me what you would like to know. We can't ruin a good meal with talk of darkness, hunting, and the death of magic. It just isn't proper."

"The death of magic?" I raised an eyebrow.

"*Oohhhh*," she said ominously.

"It doesn't sound like something you should make fun of."

"No, it's serious business." The smell of cooking filled the cottage, and my stomach rumbled. "So is attempting to fill a man's stomach, it seems. I think you've eaten an entire sheep since you've been here."

After dinner, Aileen commanded me into the living room where she installed me on a settee upholstered with a flowery fabric.

"You don't seem very serious about everything," I said, scowling.

"Believe me, I am. But if you can't have a laugh every once in a while, then what's the point? Fighting to live a life that's as dull as dishwater is not much of a life at all."

She had a point.

"There is much you ought to know, I suppose, but let's start with me. I used to like being the center of attention once upon a time, but the times they are a changing. Who I am has much more to do with the state of things than you would realize at first. The witches and this place...and others like it."

"Were you born here?" I asked.

"Aye, I was born right here in Derrydun," she said. "The Crescent Witches have called these lands home for longer than any can remember, but I never liked it. Not back then. The world was changing,

Ireland was in turmoil, and out there, everything was shiny...and like a magpie, I wanted it all. I was determined to rebel and go against tradition, so when I turned eighteen, I ran off and traveled the world. I was in Australia when I met my husband." She got a faraway look in her eyes, and a sad smile pulled at her lips. "Jonathan was a good man. He was human and had no idea I was a witch. None at all. It was refreshing being normal, you see. No pomp and tradition to worry about. He adored the ground I walked on, and we were very happy together. We lived by the beach in a little house with a veranda that overlooked the water. All hours of the day and night, we could sit there and watch giant cargo ships sail in and out of the bay. When storms swept over, we could see the clouds billow for miles and miles."

"Where is he now? Your husband?" I asked, wondering if he'd found out Aileen's secret and cast her out. Perhaps he didn't accept what she was.

"Still there, I suppose."

"Do you think about him?"

"Always." She glanced away but not before I saw the tears in her eyes. "We even had a daughter together. After I had given birth to her, I knew she would develop the same abilities. She did, and I wasn't expecting how strong she would be even as small as she was, so to protect her, I bound her powers. I knew it was wrong. I regretted keeping her heritage from her, but I thought it was best. We were away from the coven, Jonathan didn't know, and we were alone. When she turned two, I received word that..." She trailed off, her voice breaking.

I didn't have to have a memory to understand the Crescent Witches were set upon, their magic drained, and their lives lost. It was written all over Aileen's face. She was the last and her daughter...

"I had to come back and leave my little family behind," she went on. "To keep them safe. There are creatures out there that feed on magic, and they're getting stronger. Every year, there are less and less witches and magic...Well, there mightn't be any left before long. That's why it's so important to keep ourselves hidden. Those creatures would latch onto her like a parasite, draining every last scrap of life from her little body, and Jonathan...I couldn't bring that down upon them."

"I'm sorry," I said.

"Never you mind," she replied. "It wasn't your fault. It is what it is. It's not much consolation, but at least the Crescents live on, and our magic is still in this world."

"Your daughter?"

"Skye," she murmured. "She's still alive, none the wiser, believing I'm a terrible mother for abandoning her, but at least she's safe from all this. There's that, I suppose. She was twenty-seven this year. Twenty-seven... She must be beautiful."

"Duty," I murmured, looking into the fire. It was a familiar word, and the thought of it stirred feelings I couldn't pinpoint. I wondered if it had anything to do with my past. Thinking on it and attempting to unravel the mystery, a now familiar resistance cropped up, and pushing too far, my mind slammed into it like a psychic brick wall.

I winced and pressed my thumbs against my temples, rubbing slow circles. The motion seemed to help soothe the ache, but my mind was still locked.

"The more you try to remember, the more it'll hurt," Aileen said, wagging her finger. "Stop poking at it."

"I can't," I said with a groan. "I have to know. Where did I come from? Why were those animals chasing me? Who am I?"

Aileen hissed and rolled her eyes, looking torn.

"Can you do something?" I asked, prodding at her. "Is there some spell that could take this darkness away?"

"I'm not entirely sure. It depends on how your mind was tampered with. Either way, it's not a nice thing to go through. Perhaps not remembering is kinder."

I fisted my hands around the arm of the chair, my fingers aching.

"That's enough of that!" Aileen cried. "Stop destroying my furniture!"

Pulling my hands away, I gasped as I saw the claws that had grown from my fingertips. My fingers had elongated and curved as my hands formed into the talons of a gyrfalcon. Then I'd dug them into the upholstery of my rescuer's settee.

"I'm sorry," I muttered. "I didn't…" I'd begun to change and hadn't even realized it was happening.

"Oh, dear," she said, clucking her tongue. "What a rogue you are."

"Look at what I am," I declared, holding up my hands and brandishing my talons. "I can't even control this! This is who I am, and I don't even know I'm doing it! Were those wolves and ravens… Were they shapeshifters, too? If they come back, how can I fight them? Why do they want to kill me? *Why?*"

"Calm down, Boone," Aileen said, placing her hand on my knee. "Calm yourself before you change entirely. I can't have an angry falcon flapping about my living room."

"Can you fix my mind?" I asked, heaving a sigh of relief as my claws began to ease back into human shaped fingers.

"I can't say."

"Will you try?"

"I can, but it will hurt. A great deal, I'm afraid." She pursed her lips. "Are you sure? You only landed in the forest a night ago."

"Yes, I'm sure."

"Then we must go to the tree," she said. "You may have lost your memory for a reason. Uncovering it may be the last thing you need."

"I've thought about nothing else," I said, my brow creasing. "I may have asked someone to take it, I may be protecting something of my own, I may be protecting someone I care about, or someone may have stolen it. How am I to know which is true?"

"Aye, you have a point. It's a flawed plan— amnesia—because everyone craves an identity. Who we are is everything we are if you get my meaning."

"I don't see that I have any other choice."

Aileen grimaced, but she waved her hand. "All right. Let me put on my shoes, then we'll go to the hawthorn."

"Thank you," I said as she rose to her feet.

"Don't be thanking me yet. You may be cursing the day I was born before long."

I doubted it, but I didn't tell her that. As she disappeared into the hall, I hoped her magic could unlock something, *anything*, that could shed some light on who I was.

The forest was dark as we made our way toward the ancient hawthorn.

The wet, earthy scent permeated my senses as the closeness of the trees and the wildness of the place put me on edge. It felt as if a hundred pairs of eyes were glued to my back, and I instantly thought of the ravens. Peering over my shoulder, I could see nothing but the trees and ferns we'd already passed. We were alone.

As with the previous night, I could hear bubbling water off in the distance. It must be much deeper into the wilderness past the clearing that held the hawthorn.

Stepping into the clearing, Aileen nodded toward the hawthorn. "Can you feel it?"

I stared up at it, noticing how tall it was compared to the one in the village. It must be a thousand years old to have grown into the dominant thing it was now. Even in the dark of night, I could pick out the colors. Its leaves were a rich emerald, the berries on its boughs red as blood, and its branches knotted and snarled.

I nodded. "The air feels close. I didn't notice it last night."

"I doubt you noticed much of anything," she quipped. "That closeness you feel? That's the tree's protection. Whatever spell I cast here will be kept hidden, but only as long as we remain under her canopy."

I stepped closer, casting my gaze up as the branches stretched above my head, and the air thickened even more.

"Kneel," Aileen commanded. "Place your palms against the roots, and open yourself up to the magic in her old bones."

The notion that a tree held magic seemed absurd, but I'd felt something come from it the night before as I did now. Warmth, safety, and something else. Placing my knees into a hollow at the base of the trunk, I grasped the exposed roots and bowed my head.

Aileen stood behind me, her hands on my shoulders, and I tensed.

"This is going to sting a little," she warned. "Try to hold still."

"Do what you need to," I replied, bracing myself.

"All right. You asked for it."

At first, I felt her magic trickle into my mind, her hands warm on my shoulders. Slowly, the darkness began to shift...then pain tore through my mind like a hundred hot pokers stabbing into my flesh. Over and over, biting, burning *agony*.

A woman cried out from far away, and all at once, the connection was severed. Shoved forward into the tree by a silent explosion of air, I grunted, smacking the top of my head against the trunk. Dazed, I turned just in time to see Aileen fly across the clearing. With a wallop, she hit a pile of leaves, and they flew into the air, fluttering everywhere.

Scrambling to my feet, I sprinted to her, my heart beating frantically. My head throbbed something fierce, but it was nothing compared to the alarm that overcame me at the sight of Aileen in full flight.

I kneeled, scraping leaves away from her face, and dug her out.

"Are you all right?" I asked as she blinked up at me.

"*Wowee!*" she cried. "What a kick!"

I frowned, not expecting her reaction at all. From the way she'd flown across the clearing, I thought she would be bruised and battered, but it looked like she was high as a kite.

"What happened?" I asked. "You look..."

"Whatever happened to you, it's strong," she said, sitting up. "Your mind is locked tighter than Fort Knox!"

"What's a Fort Knox?"

"A really big vault that's impossible to get into," she explained. "I'm afraid there's no getting inside there." She tapped my forehead.

I fell back onto my ass and cursed, rubbing my hands over my face. "So I'll never know who I am?"

"I didn't say that."

"Then how can I unlock this Fort Knox?"

"It's not a Fort Knox... That's just a metaphor." Aileen sighed and started picking leaf litter from her hair. "I would say the only way you're getting your memories back is by finding whoever locked them up in the first place. That kind of magic comes with a signature, like a combination."

I cursed again, this time growling my frustration to the sky. It came out a little too animal like for Aileen's liking, and she flinched.

The only way I was finding out who I was was finding someone I couldn't remember to undo the spell they'd put on my mind. I was stuck, and I knew it, and so did Aileen. There was no quick fix to this. Realistically, there might not be one at all.

This? My rebirth as Boone—the shapeshifter who couldn't control his changes, the man who didn't know his heritage, and the man without a home—might be it.

I was hunted by a dark power I didn't understand, and the only place I was safe seemed to be Derrydun with its mystical ancient hawthorn tree. I knew to come here, so what did that mean? The moment I left to search for answers, they could find me again. This was it. This place, this person I'd woken up as... This was it.

I couldn't leave. I was stuck here. Probably forever.

"Come," Aileen said gently. "Let's go home."

"Home?" I whispered, feeling completely lost.

"To be sure," she declared. "Where else are you going to go?"

CHAPTER 5

A week passed, and I'd resigned myself to building a new life in Derrydun.

Under the protection of the hawthorn, I was free to come and go as I pleased, helping Aileen with her garden and shop. We continued the ruse that I was nothing more than the son of an old friend of hers, and just like that, I was now a resident of the village.

I didn't know who or what was after me so I couldn't leave, and Aileen knew about my abilities, so she could help me come to terms with what I was. Like a child, it seemed, I had to learn everything all over again. Instinct was one thing, controlling what happened in front of a bunch of people who didn't know magic existed was another.

Like clockwork, I'd taken to sitting with Aileen in her shop every morning before prowling the forest of an afternoon. I couldn't go far—I wasn't sure where the boundary of the hawthorn's magic ended —but it was far enough.

I watched Aileen shuffle her tarot cards. She hadn't asked me to draw another, and I hadn't felt the need to with the message she'd given me that first day. *Stabbed in the back.* I had been, but besides the ravens, it could be the reason why my memories were locked away.

I winced, a sharp spike of pain splitting through my head, and Aileen narrowed her eyes at me. Her look said everything.

Turning to the counter, she placed the cards facedown and swept them across the surface in a long arc. She peered at them for a moment, then reached out and drew one from the left side.

Turning it over, she sighed and set it down in front of her.

"You always draw the same one," I said, placing my finger on the card. "What is it?"

"The Tower."

"What does it mean?"

"A variety of things," she replied. "So much has happened this last week, I was entirely positive it was pointing at your arrival, but now I'm not so sure."

"Because it keeps coming up?"

"Precisely." Aileen smiled and pulled the cards back into a neat pile. "The Tower looks like a frightening card with its crumbling tower and storm clouds, but it's actually quite positive. Tarot is like that, and so is the world. Nothing is what it seems."

"It reminds me of the tower house on the hill," I murmured, thinking of the crumbling ruin that loomed over Derrydun.

"If you travel deeper into the forest, you'll find more ruins," Aileen declared. "The tower house was once part of a sprawling estate built over lands that were once home to the ancient peoples of Ireland. The entire area is full of magical places and stories that would warm your heart and make your toes curl at the evils that live in our world."

"How far can I go before the hawthorn's protection ends?" I asked.

"The hawthorn in the forest stretches at least a few miles, and the one here in the village perhaps a mile," she replied. "Why do you ask?"

I shrugged. "Perhaps I should make myself useful if I'm going to be stuck here."

"I know it's not ideal, but it is what it is. Things tend to happen for a reason, you know."

"I can't sit around and wallow in my misfortune," I said, glancing out the shop window. Another busload of tourists had just navigated the hawthorn down the road and was pulling into the coach bay beside Mary's Teahouse. "Besides, you clothe and feed me and ask for nothing. I may have lost my identity, but I haven't lost my strength."

Aileen snorted. "If you want some work, there's plenty of it around here. Maybe it's not such a bad idea."

"There is a bus coming," I said. "Do you want me to stay?"

"I can manage. Mairead should be here soon enough."

Leaving Aileen with her tarot cards, I ventured out into Derrydun to start building a semblance of a life. If this was to be my home, then I had to make it into something I could tolerate. Filling my days with work would mean less time inflicting myself with headaches trying to puzzle out my past.

I set out with fierce determination, and by the end of the day, I'd negotiated duties and payment at several shops and also up on the farm overlooking the village. I was to help three nights a week in the kitchen at Molly McCreedy's, and I'd offered to tend to old Mrs. Boyle's garden and trim her hedges once a month. I was to fetch the local produce deliveries for Mary at the Teahouse, and I was the new farmhand on Roy O'Toole's property on the hill behind Aileen's cottage.

It was simple and lonely work, but I would be close to nature where I felt the safest, and well within the boundary of the hawthorns.

Molly McCreedy's had been my last stop, so I pulled up a stool by the bar. It was a tiny little place, full of the scent of stale barley and hops as well as the lingering perfumes of cooking from the kitchen beyond. Behind the counter was a set of taps with large handles. I watched the barmaid pull down on one and fill a glass with beer, the top frothing as the golden liquid reached the rim.

"Ye want one?" a man asked from beside me. "My shout."

"Sure," I replied, looking him over. "Why not?"

"You're Boone, the lad staying with Aileen, right?"

I nodded. "I am."

"I hear ye are goin' to be workin' with Roy." He held out his hand. "Sean McKinnon."

Slapping my palm in his, we shook. We seemed to be around the same age, though Sean was well worn around the edges. His face bore the lines of exhaustion, his beard was scrappy, and his clothes were slightly rumpled. He also had the ingrained smell of alcohol around him, which didn't bode well.

"Yes, I start tomorrow," I replied.

"Have ye worked with sheep before?"

"No, but I have a way with animals," I said. A literal way considering I could break all the bones in my body and change into them at will.

"There's naught much to it," he said, his thick

accent almost musical. "I can teach ye how to whistle to Phee, and she be doin' all the leg work."

"Phee?"

"The border collie. Smart as a tack for a dog, and to think she was the runt of the litter."

His words evoked a familiarity to me, and I frowned, shaking off the sensation before my head burst in the middle of the pub.

"Here you go." The woman behind the bar placed a pint of beer down in front of me, her red lips smiling broadly at me. Her eyelashes fluttered. She was quite pretty with her red hair, freckled cheeks, and slender frame, but romance was the furthest thing from my mind.

"Stop makin' eyes at him, Hannah," Sean complained. "You know my heart burns for ye."

"Sean, stop it with your blabberin'," she said with a groan. "You're drunk. You know what that means."

"Aye. Time to go home." He slammed his empty glass onto the bar and held out his hand to me. "Nice to be meetin' ye, Boone. I'll see you on the farm."

"Sure," I said, shaking on it. As he stumbled off, he bumped against a table, then immediately sat in a chair by the door.

"He lost his wife a few weeks ago," Hannah explained as I sipped on my beer. "Cancer, the poor girl. She was a real beauty. Sean's been a fixture around here ever since."

"He's not handling it very well?" I asked, assuming he was self-medicating his loss with alcohol.

"Yes and no. Sometimes, he's bright as can be, but other times, he's just lost, you know?" Hannah glanced across the bar and frowned. Following her gaze, I saw Sean had slumped in his chair and had begun snoring loudly. "He comes here so he's not alone, I think. We look out for him, but there's only so much we can do."

I raised an eyebrow. "You might have to start cutting him off."

"Oh, I see how it is," she declared, pouting. "One week in Derrydun, and you know how it is. Where did you come from to know all there is about these parts, eh?"

"Do you want me to take Sean home?" I said, blatantly avoiding her questioning. "He's starting to drool."

Hannah narrowed her eyes. "If you like."

Standing, I brushed off my trousers. "Where does he live?"

"Half a mile along the main road to your right. The farmhouse just past the bend. On the fence near the gate, you'll see the name of the house, Ashmere. That's the one you be looking for."

"Thanks." Approaching Sean, I wondered if I could carry him. I seemed to have a great deal of strength, but I wasn't sure it extended to drunken Irishmen.

"Boone?"

Turning at the sound of Hannah's voice, I raised an eyebrow.

"Thank you. He's impossible to move when he passes out. I was afraid I would find him asleep in Mrs. Boyle's flowers again. She was beating him with a broom, and he still wouldn't move."

Smiling, I nodded. "You're welcome."

Giving him a shake, Sean's eyes opened, and he started muttering to himself.

"Time to go home," I said, pulling him to his feet.

Giving one last wave to Hannah, we left the empty pub and started the walk, his arm slung over my shoulder while I propped him up. We must've been a comical sight, stumbling down the side of the road in the dark, but Derrydun was a sleepy little place, and there was no one around to witness it.

As we approached the farmhouse, my skin began to itch and prickle. Pausing to rest a moment, Sean moaned, his breath stinking of beer.

"Are we there yet?" he asked.

"We're just outside," I replied. "Do you see?"

He peered up at his house. "Oh, yeah. That's the one."

Glancing at the forest behind the farmhouse, I was sure something lingered just past the rise. Hoisting Sean up, I guided him down the path to the front door of his house, and he leaned against the wall, completely out of his mind.

Everything felt electrified as if a storm was brewing on the horizon, but I knew there was no bad weather coming. Not in the sky at least. The harder I focused on the presence, the more my skin prickled. It tugged at me like a magnet attracting metal, and I turned, staring into the darkness. There was something there, calling to me. Something...

Sean moaned and began rattling at the door. "It's locked," he cried. "Justine! Let me in, woman! *Justine!*"

Shaking off the odd sensation, I turned back to Sean, assuming Justine had been his wife.

"She's not here," I said, patting his coat pockets looking for his house keys.

"You're Boone," he said, slurring his words.

"That I am."

"You're staying with Aileen."

"Yes." Finding the keys, I began trying each in the door until I found the right one. The lock clicked, and I let us into the house. "Can you find your way to bed?"

"Go, go," Sean said, waving his hand at me. "I'll be fine."

Not wanting to linger a moment longer, I let him be, leaving behind the farmhouse and the weird pull toward the forest.

Outside, the darkness was soothing, the air seeming to dilute the effects of whatever was lingering just outside of my awareness. Worried it might have something to do with the things that were hunting me or even the parasites Aileen had mentioned were searching for her, I hurried back to the village.

The lights were still on in the cottage when I finally crossed into the garden, and inside, I found the witch sitting in her favorite armchair, knitting some unknown article of clothing. Her fingers worked the needles with expert precision, and she didn't even drop a stitch when she looked up at me.

"I hear you've been busy," she said as I stood in the doorway.

"I have. I'm sorry I'm late."

Aileen screwed up her nose. "No need to apologize to me. I'm not your mother."

I began to wonder who was, and a now familiar headache erupted in my brain.

"You need to work on that," the witch said, resuming her knitting. "You might blow your brain to smithereens."

"I was at the pub," I said. "I took Sean McKinnon home..."

"Aye? He lost his wife a few weeks back." She clucked her tongue. "Such a lovely woman."

"So I hear..."

Setting down her knitting needles, Aileen peered up at me. "What else did you find?"

"Err..." I wasn't sure how she knew, but her intuition was starting to become annoying.

"Well then, spit it out."

"Beyond Sean's farmhouse," I began. "Something was..."

"Ah, there's another hawthorn down there," Aileen explained. "That's likely what you felt. Like a tingling, yes? A magnet pulling at your skin?"

I nodded. "Yeah."

"All creatures of magic are drawn to such places," she went on. "It's normal to sense them, but it's not always wise to seek them out."

"Why? If it's only a hawthorn..."

"They're never *just a hawthorn*," she said with a pout.

I frowned but didn't continue my questioning. It was late, and I had an early morning if I wanted to be on time for my first day working on Roy's farm. Still, I was curious. If it were only a hawthorn, the tree that protected our kind, then why would she warn me away? I had no idea.

I had turned, intending to go to bed, when Aileen called out.

"Boone?"

I glanced over my shoulder and waited.

"Don't go looking for trouble, you hear? It never ends well."

"No," I murmured, still thinking about the strange magic that lingered past Sean McKinnon's house. "I won't."

CHAPTER 6

Roy was a robust man in his early sixties. His belly was round, his cheeks were red, and he didn't seem to give a hoot about anything.

We were sitting on a bale of hay, watching a truck reverse into the yard. A dozen or so sheep were loaded in the back, bleating and stamping their feet on the tray as the driver went over a bump. A black and white border collie was running laps around the entire scene, biting at the wheels and barking in excitement.

Roy whistled sharply at the dog. "Phee! C'mere!"

Phee did another lap and came toward us, her tongue lolling happily. The moment she saw me sitting there, she bounded straight up to me, sat at my feet, and nudged my leg with her snout until I placed my palm on her head.

"You've got a way about ye," Roy said, scratching his head. "She's in love."

"At least someone is," I said wryly, earning myself a laugh from the old man.

Handing me a can of blue spray paint, he nodded toward the truck. The driver had started unloading sheep into the paddock by the gate, the pungent stench of wet wool filling the air as their hooves churned the earth beneath them.

"What's this for?" I asked.

"Spray a little line on their asses," he declared. "We've got four lots of sheep runnin' across that hill, and we need to tell 'em apart. That bugger McGregor tried to pinch me best ewe last summer by paintin' over her. We kicked him out and lost his money, but even so, it was still cheaper than buildin' a mile of drywall to separate them out."

One thing I was fast learning was that while not shy when it came to hard work, if the Irish didn't have to do it, then they made it their mission not to.

I climbed over the fence and landed in the yard, mud squelching under my boots. The sheep spooked and headed for the opposite side of the pen. In the background, Phee began to bark, disappointed she wasn't allowed in on the action.

Letting my instincts take over, I dove for the closest ewe, grasped her neck, and sprayed a neat line over her rump. Seeing I'd missed a spot, I filled it in before letting her go.

"You don't need to paint a bloody Rembrandt!" Roy bellowed. "Just spray 'em!"

Grimacing, I darted about the yard, slipping and sliding while Roy and the truck driver bellowed with laughter. The sheep were slippery, and their flighty nature made them experts in the art of evasion. Fortunate for them, but not for me. Eventually, I managed to mark them all without falling on my ass in the mud. I would call that a win and some welcome entertainment for the men.

Vaulting over the fence, I handed Roy back the can of spray paint.

"Not bad for ye first go," he said. "Where did ye come from, anyhoo? Ye a city lad?"

I shrugged, unsure what tale to spin. I couldn't exactly tell him I was a fox in my spare time.

"You're a man of few words. Be careful. People oft like to jump to conclusions about that."

"I fell on hard times, is all," I said, filling in the gap as much as I could. "I needed a place to call home, and Aileen offered to help."

Roy eyed me. "She's a good judge of character, our Aileen."

"She is."

"Ye better not be thinkin' about causin' any trouble around here," he said sternly.

"I don't plan on giving you any."

We watched the sheep mill about for a few minutes, standing side by side. When Sean's car came into view, the old man waved me away.

"Go with Sean," he said. "He'll show ye the limits of the property and take ye to see the cows. Keep an eye out for Bully. He's a mean bugger."

Thanking the old man, I went to meet Sean. When he got out of his car, I saw he was a sight cleaner in his jeans, flannel, and boots, but his eyes were red, betraying the raging hangover he must've woken with.

"Hey, Boone," he said.

"Sean." I nodded.

"Thank ye for last night," he said, clapping me on the shoulder. "I know I was a right eejit. I suppose Hannah explained everythin' to ye?"

"She did," I replied. "Don't worry about it."

"Gettin' drunk isn't goin' to help, but I can't stop myself."

"Time heals most wounds, I suppose." I glanced at the sky and spied a falcon soaring above. Focusing on it, I began to feel the same pull I had the night before, but this time, my bones began to vibrate.

"I suppose you're right," Sean replied bringing my attention down to earth. "Now come with me, and we'll go see Bully. If ye are as good with animals as ye say ye are, then it'll be a right treat, that."

"Roy already warned me about Bully," I said with a smirk.

"Darn it!" he cursed as we crossed the yard.

Smiling, I thumped him on the back, grateful I'd already made a friend.

After that, I settled into my new life in Derrydun with ease. With plenty of work to keep me occupied, I had little time to dwell on my past, which meant I almost completely stopped giving myself splitting headaches.

I hadn't realized it, but that first day on the farm, the falcon I'd seen flying above us had been calling to the magic inside of me. The animals I changed into were just as much a part of who I was as my original human form, and I was fast learning I had to change before I was forced to. It seemed staying human forever was not an option.

Every other night, I went to the ancient hawthorn in the forest and changed, spending hours in the darkness running as a fox or flying as a gyrfalcon.

And every time I circled Derrydun, I still felt the pull of the mysterious hawthorn in the glade behind Sean McKinnon's farmhouse. Heeding Aileen's warning, I stayed away, but it was becoming increasingly hard to ignore the buzzing every time I sat in the field overlooking the village as I was now.

Perched on the drywall, I surveyed the scene that had become more familiar to me than my own face. The rolling green hills, the steely blue smudge of the ocean on the horizon, the snaking roads that cut across the countryside, and the roofs of the buildings that made up the village. Roy's sheep chewed happily on the grass before me, and beyond that, I could see the shingles on Sean's farmhouse. Even further, I could sense the place of power—the hawthorn—its magic hitting me in sickly waves.

I couldn't take it anymore.

Deciding to investigate before I lost my mind, I cast my gaze over the field. No one was around. In the distance, the droning of Roy's tractor could be heard as he rumbled across the far field, and Phee's excited barking followed. Sean was away at the market, so that meant I was completely alone and free to slip away for an hour.

My bones popped, cracking and shrinking into the delicate framework of my most familiar form. The gyrfalcon. My sweater began to billow around me, becoming too large for my shoulders, and my trousers fell down, my hips no longer able to hold them up. Feeling my eyes bubble and morph and my beak sprout, my world shifted as the animal took over.

Burrowing out of my clothes, I hopped onto the edge of the drywall and shook out my feathers. Preening, I sat for a moment, becoming accustomed to my form. Changing was becoming more familiar now, and the pain was lessening the more I practiced. I no longer felt like throwing up when I regained my human shape, so I took it as a good sign.

Leaping, I stretched out my wings and flapped. Wind buffeted around me as my senses picked up on the air currents, and I soared higher and higher.

Wheeling over the farmhouse, I let my senses guide me. The closer I ventured, the more my stomach rolled, and before long, I was able to pick out the hawthorn from the other trees around it.

At first, I couldn't see anything amiss, but as I circled lower, I zeroed in on a dark shadow at the base of the tree. It appeared to be digging where the trunk met the earth, and dirt was flying everywhere. The pull of magic was strengthening, and I wondered if this was what I'd been feeling the past week. Was the hawthorn calling for help?

The more I pondered it, the more it didn't make sense for Aileen to warn me away. The better course of action was to protect the tree and not let this thing —whatever it was—harm it.

Circling lower still, I studied the creature. It was a man-shaped thing, but it wore no clothes, and there were no shoes on its feet. Its body was covered in a thick charcoal hide, its clawed hands tipped with mean looking talons that ripped and tore at the base of the hawthorn. The sounds of intelligible muttering reached me even at this height, and my heart began to beat faster. Whatever it was, it was definitely not from this world. Even I was smart enough to understand that.

Landing on a branch overlooking the hawthorn, I watched the creature, my falcon eyes able to see much clearer than my human ones.

The moment I settled, its head shot up, and it turned, its beady black eyes searching the glade. Sharp, pointed teeth protruded behind its lips as it sniffed the air, and I began to feel uneasy.

The instant its gaze hit mine, it let out an unearthly roar and ran across the clearing. It leapt, colliding with the tree, and I was dislodged. Flapping my wings, I cried out, the sound echoing through the glade as I tumbled to the ground.

A gnarled hand clamped around my middle and pinned my wings to my sides. I wriggled, pecking and clawing in a desperate attempt to free myself, but I was stuck.

"Magic," it said forcefully. "*Magic!*"

"Let him go!"

I screeched, digging my beak into the creature's flesh. A gust of wind collided with us, and we were sent flying, the grip around my body slackening enough so I could wriggle free.

That was when I realized Aileen stood at the edge of the glade, her hand raised. Magic bled from her, sending waves of heat across my body. I saw why she didn't use her power unless it was absolutely necessary. The witch shone like a beacon in the darkness, calling everything to her. The sky, the earth, and all the creatures that lived between the two.

She swept her hands in a long arc, and light filled the glade, brighter than any sun or flame. Burying my eyes under my battered wing, I heard the screams of the creature as whatever magic Aileen had flung at it, tore through its body.

Whatever happened next, I didn't know. When I peered from behind my feathers, the creature was gone, and the witch stood over me, a look of absolute rage on her face. I'd never seen her look so angry, and I cowered under the weight of it.

Aileen grabbed me by the scruff of the neck and shook me with all her might. The force of her anger caused my bones to shatter, and I began to change back into a man. Fire tore through my body as my limbs lengthened and my insides grew, my white feathers melting into my flesh.

When I was done, I knelt in the dirt, naked as the day I was born. I was ashamed to look up. I knew what I would find if I did. Disappointment. I'd gone looking for trouble and had almost been killed, and Aileen...she had almost been dragged down with me.

I wasn't a warrior or a savior.

I was a fool.

CHAPTER 7

"What did I tell you?" Aileen exclaimed.

"I'm sorry," I muttered. "I didn't think it would be a worry if I was a gyrfalcon."

"That's right," she seethed. "You didn't think."

The witch muttered under her breath and began pacing back and forth in front of me.

"The hawthorn was hurting, wasn't it?" I asked. "That's what I was feeling."

"You were lucky I was watching it," Aileen said irritably.

"Why didn't you tell me?"

Her expression contorted, and I was positive she didn't trust me quite as much as she'd let on. If she did, she would've told me the truth about the hawthorn when I asked about it the other night. Then we wouldn't be in this predicament.

"It was a craglorn," she declared, avoiding my question. "A servant of the witch Carman."

"Who?" I narrowed my eyes. I was tired of not understanding the world I was a part of. Not because I was daft but because I couldn't remember.

"A power hungry bitch, that's who. Evil to the core. She did some very bad things and was banished from Ireland over a thousand years ago because of it. There's no way she can return. Ohh, I can see that look in your eyes. She ought to be dead after that long, right? Not her. Not with the magic she's sucked out of witches all over the world. She wants back in, laddy, and she will stop at nothing to open the doorways to the fae realm."

I stared up at her, not understanding. Fae realm?

"The fae realm," Aileen reiterated, rolling her eyes. "The land of magic and creatures stranger than you and I put together. A thousand years ago, the doorways were sealed. Just like that." She clapped her hands together, the sound echoing through the glade. "People and creatures were trapped on both sides. Who knows what's happening over there, but here..." She shook her head. "Those parasites I told you about? They're dying without magic, flapping around like fish out of water. That's where we come in." She made a slurping sound. "We're fish food, Boone. Magic is the key to opening the doorways, but none of us have enough on our own. Together, though..."

That thing—the craglorn—and others like it were trapped and had resorted to killing, feeding, and sucking the life out of this world in a desperate attempt to stay alive. It had grabbed me the moment it sensed my magic. It had been desperate, its black eyes empty.

Aileen turned and stared at the hawthorn. "Who knows what horrors will come out of there if Carman gets her way. There are enough of them here already."

Glancing at the tree, I began to piece together the puzzle. The craglorn had been scratching at the base of the hawthorn, and the only thing left behind was the hole it had managed to dig among the roots.

"The doorways," I began. "They're guarded by the hawthorns, aren't they?"

"Aye," Aileen said, some of the anger disappearing from her voice.

"Will they come now?" I asked. "Other craglorns?"

"I hope not," Aileen replied. "The tree should still be strong enough to have dampened my signature, though this one is not long for this world."

"The hawthorn has that kind of magic? I thought..."

"Of course, it does. All of them do to varying

degrees. When the Crescent Witches were at the height of their power, they used them to hold their councils. Under the branches of a hawthorn, words are protected, doorway or no. As you know, there was a reason you landed underneath one the night I found you."

Covering myself, I sat on the grass, my mind turning over. I felt sick to the stomach. Mostly because I'd betrayed the one person who'd placed their complete trust in me, but also because I was starting to believe I may have been targeting the hawthorn because I was also trying to go home. I had a human body, but I was a shapeshifter. What if this wasn't who I was at all? What if under my skin was the stony hide of a creature like the craglorn? Was that why she didn't trust me?

Aileen sat beside me, her gaze locked on the hawthorn. "Things are going to get a lot worse before they have a chance of getting better," she said. "I'm not sure I can protect Derrydun on my own, let alone face Carman."

"Aren't there other witches?"

"There are, but they're all in hiding. Who knows how to find any of them. If a witch doesn't want to be found, then it's near impossible to find her."

"Can I help?"

She studied my expression for a moment and then sighed. "I've seen enough of your bare ass to last a lifetime. You had better flap away and find where you left your clothes."

"But—"

"Roy will be wondering where you are." She rose to her feet gracefully and approached the hawthorn.

While her back was turned, I changed back into a gyrfalcon and flew up onto a branch. I watched her examine the damage the craglorn had inflicted on the tree, but she never raised her head.

I flew off toward the farm, my heart heavy. I didn't belong in the human world, and I didn't belong with the supernatural. The secrets were starting to pile up, and I didn't like it, not one bit. The creature, the truth behind who was stealing magic, the doorways to the fae realm, my hidden nature... What if I had something to do with it all?

Below, the farm came into view, and I spied Roy and his tractor crossing the far field, making for the yard. Reaching the spot where I'd changed, I landed and returned to my human form.

Lacing my boots back up, I began to feel a sharp pain in my back. The more I dwelled on what I'd learned, the more uncomfortable I became.

The Ten of Swords. Thinking about the tarot card I'd drawn my first morning in Derrydun, the more I believed its message.

Betrayed by a power that has no mercy or feeling...

For the first time since I began remembering, the sky was clear.

Sitting in the garden behind the cottage, I gazed up at the stars, studying the silver points of light. There was no moon, and it only made them shine brighter, the universe infinite compared to my insignificant life.

Wracked with guilt and worry, I hadn't ventured inside. I could still see the craglorn in my mind's eye, its hideous black eyes etched in my memory for eternity. Definitely not one I wanted to keep. My ribs ached, and I rubbed my palm against my chest. Maybe it was time to find somewhere new to live.

Behind me, I heard the kitchen door open and close.

"Are you coming inside, or are you going to sleep with the carrots?" Aileen asked, standing over me.

"The carrots seem nice," I muttered.

She sighed dramatically and sat on the grass beside me. "I keep forgetting you're a man and not a boy."

I stared at my hands. "I'm not sure whether to be offended by that or not."

"You may have forgotten your past, but you haven't forgotten how to live."

"But I've forgotten magic..."

Aileen lifted her chin and peered at the stars.

"I spoke to Mrs. Boyle this afternoon," she said after a moment.

I snorted. Old Mrs. Boyle, the crazy women who lived along the main road and scared away children who dared come too close to her fence with her broom. I knew there was anger in her, whether it was from a past hurt or something else, I didn't know, but she seemed to tolerate my presence. I trimmed her hedges and pulled the weeds from her garden beds, then she handed me thirty euros. I couldn't see what she had to do with any of my stupid decisions.

"I've never heard her speak so highly of anyone in my life," Aileen went on. "What did you say to her?"

"Nothing," I replied, wondering where this was going. "I just tended to her garden as promised."

"Hmm," the witch said thoughtfully. "When I was a girl, she frightened off a con man who was doing the rounds of the village. No one suspected a thing, and he almost took off with the life savings of a few residents. Before he left, he decided to tangle with Mrs. Boyle. I never knew what happened, but he ran off with his tail between his legs, and the local constable chasing after him down the road. The next day, everyone got their money back."

"What does that have to do with me?" I asked sullenly.

"Mrs. Boyle has an impeccable eye when it comes to shady characters."

"Did I come from there?" I murmured, placing my palms on the earth.

"Where?" Aileen sounded surprised I'd even asked.

"The hawthorn..."

"From the fae realm?" she asked, aghast. "Of course not. Why would you think something like that?"

I lowered my head, my unruly hair covering my eyes.

"Boone, like me, you're human. The only difference is you were born with magic in you. That's all."

My shoulders sank in relief, but my heart was still heavy.

"There's more worrying you," she said.

"Do you trust me?" I asked straight out.

"Of course, I do. What kind of question is that?"

"If you do, then why didn't you tell me the truth about the hawthorns? You could've told me everything, and I wouldn't have..." I hissed and turned away. "I wouldn't have forced you to reveal your magic to half the parasites in Ireland."

"It is what it is."

I couldn't accept her answers. Everything she said came with ten different meanings. She explained her reasons yet left out everything that mattered, expecting me to be okay with it. Was it a witch trait or something more?

"Why can I help you?" I asked. "If the hawthorn isn't strong enough to hide what you did today, then more of the things could turn up."

"I've been protecting Derrydun for a long time," she replied. "I know what I need to do, and you... You need to settle and come to terms with who you are before you think about becoming more."

"But you said you might not be able to protect the village on your own."

"Perhaps not indefinitely, but I won't allow it to come to that. We are only human under all the supernatural, after all. I won't force you before you're ready, Boone."

"I'm a full-grown man, yet I feel like a child," I said sharply. "I don't belong, I don't understand, and I don't remember. I can't get past it. All these jobs I've been doing are just bollocks. A stupid distraction. I'm make-believe, Aileen. Even my name isn't real."

"Bollocks?" Aileen asked with a snort. "Mrs. Boyle can finally see her garden path thanks to you, and she's a sight friendlier. It's been a week and counting since she's chased a child with her broom of doom. Roy values your hard work and likes that he doesn't have to tell you what to do, that you just do it. The animals flock to you like bees to honey, and that farm has never run smoother. Mary is free to expand her business because you've taken over her deliveries and don't charge her a premium. Everyone at the pub is happier, and all you do is wash dirty plates and glasses. You show Mairead a little kindness every so often, and now she doesn't hate everything anymore and is nicer to my customers. And Sean McKinnon has been fifty percent less drunk since you've become friends." She looked at me with a raised eyebrow. "None of that is bollocks, Boone."

I scowled, and she lifted her hand and slapped me on the back of the head.

"*Ow!* What was that for?" I rubbed my palm against my skull.

"You're being a selfish little toad," she declared. "*Boohoo*, you can't remember your past because someone locked your memories away and threw away the key. Toughen up, Boone. You're alive, among new friends who actually care, and you're safe. You made a mistake today. Am I angry? You bet I am, but we'll get over it. Stop dwelling on the things you can't change and worry about those you can." She jabbed a finger toward the village. "Those people matter, and so do you."

A wave of nausea swept over me, and I bowed my head. She was right. I'd retreated into myself, and all I could think about was the bad things that had happened to me. I thought I'd tried, but I hadn't at all.

"Would you draw another card for me?" I asked, pulling at the grass.

Aileen placed her hand on mine to stop me destroying her lawn. "I thought you didn't believe in them."

I shrugged. "Perhaps I'm starting to convert."

She laughed softly.

"Will you?"

"Tomorrow," she said with a smile. "I think we've had enough excitement for one day, don't you?"

CHAPTER 8

Staring at the giant amethyst cave perched in a glass cabinet inside Irish Moon, I fidgeted nervously. Its energy was doing nothing to calm me, especially when I could see Aileen's reflection behind it.

As promised, she'd dragged me into her shop so she could draw me another card from her tarot deck. After the events of the last few days, I wasn't sure I was ready to see what it said about me. The first card had begun to show its meaning in more ways than I'd been expecting, and I wasn't keen on having my misdemeanors shoved into my face yet again.

"Are you ready, or are you more interested in amethyst?" Aileen called out from behind the counter.

Sighing, I turned and moved toward her as she shuffled the cards. As I sat beside her, she set the deck on the glass countertop and placed her palm over the cards before sweeping them to the side.

"You know the drill," the witch said. "Pick one that calls to you, and we'll see what it reveals."

Reaching out, I allowed my hand to hover over the fanned out cards. The gold foil design on the backs sparkled as I moved until I finally felt my fingers dragged toward one end. Choosing my card, I drew it out and set it face up on the counter.

The card held the image of an angel with two chalices, a wave of water flowing between the two. The card was upside down this time, whereas the Ten of Swords had been the right orientation.

"Temperance but reversed," Aileen said, announcing the name of the card. "Major Arcana this time."

"What does it mean?" I asked eagerly. An angel didn't seem as confronting as a man with ten swords stabbed into his back, and I hoped it was a good sign. I desperately needed one.

"It can suggest you lack a long-term purpose, and you feel unbalanced because of it," Aileen replied. "I would say that was fairly accurate, wouldn't you?"

Grunting, I nodded.

"You should probably focus on finding your happy place," she went on, explaining the meaning behind the card. "Lack of direction and meaning is causing stress and may manifest as impatience, excessiveness, or reckless behaviors. In this instance, balance is the key to finding purpose." She tilted her head to the side and made a face. "I can attest to the reckless part."

Choosing to ignore her and not dredge up yesterday's misadventure, I asked, "What kind of balance?"

Aileen shrugged. "It could mean balance in your day to day life, your ability to control and master your abilities, even your greater purpose, or it could be a mixture of them all. It's hard to say."

"So, I should think about the message and what it would mean to my current state of mind?"

The witch smiled brightly and nodded. "See, you're finally beginning to get it. Tarot isn't so bad after all, right?"

"Temperance is about balance," I mused aloud. In life, spirit, and my connection with who I was. The shapeshifter, the human, and my new identity as Boone.

"You're out of balance now, but it doesn't mean it's forever," Aileen declared.

"I have to find a purpose," I said, scratching my chin. "Maybe helping people in the village is what I'm supposed to be doing..."

"You're much stronger now," Aileen said, watching me in that witchy way she had. Like she was seeing my aura or something. "Your confidence is growing. You seem to be forming an identity."

I scowled even though I knew she was right. I wasn't sure if knowing my past would have any effect on who I was now. That man was gone, and all that was left was Boone. He was who I was now. Boone, the jack-of-all-trades, the secret shapeshifter, the mysterious man of Derrydun.

Aileen protected me, mostly from my own curiosity, but I also fancied I protected her. At least, I could someday.

"You've got today off, don't you?" she asked. When I nodded, she said, "Then why don't you go out and take a walk or fly or whatever it is you do. It's better than sitting in here all day."

"I don't mind." It was true since the horde of crystals around us were so soothing.

"I do. You're cramping my style."

Raising an eyebrow, I stared at her.

"Every time you're in here and a bus shows up, sales dip," she explained, shuffling the tarot cards absently. "All the women are too busy fawning over the ruggedly handsome Irishman and not my stock."

"Me?" I snorted.

"Yes, you." She rolled her eyes, doing her best to hide her laughter. "Get out and have some fun.

After leaving Aileen, I walked as far as I was able

through the forest before doubling back toward Derrydun.

The tower house loomed over me, and I gazed up at it as if I was seeing it for the first time. I'd flown over it dozens of times, but I'd never really stopped to look at it before now. There was no particular reason for it, but I supposed it was a part of the landscape like the forest or the village.

Approaching, I felt a tingle in the base of my spine. It might've been the thrill of discovery, or it might've been something more, there was no way to tell. My senses were kicked into overdrive. It didn't worry me, so I ventured forward, glad there was something new to be discovered within the boundary of the hawthorns.

Half of the structure had crumbled, leaving the interior open to the elements. Moss, vines, and grass had grown in every available crack, making it hard to imagine anyone had lived here at all. Further inside, I could see the distinct remains of three floors, and in the far corner, an alcove where spiral stairs had been set into the tower wall.

Surrounded by trees, it was secluded enough, and as visitors were not allowed to trample over the grounds, its wildness was beautiful. In the distance, I could hear the hum of the village, but it was almost drowned out by the comings and goings of nature. Birds sang, creatures burrowed and foraged, leaves rustled, and trees creaked. The air was close, almost as if a cone of silence had been dropped over the entire ruin, sealing me inside.

Sitting on the crumbled wall, I stared up at the sky, studying the clouds through a window right at the top. I wondered who used to live here. Ancient graffiti was carved into a stone here and there, but there was nothing left to give me a clue as to who they were.

A bellow echoed across the hill, the sound bouncing around inside the ruin. My head turned at the call, and I listened. Another sharp yell echoed over the fields, and not even the ruined walls and the strange sound barrier muffled it.

I could feel surprise, pain, and a tinge of fear... Something was happening, and it wasn't good.

Placing my palm against the wall, I gasped as an image flashed before me. I could see it as plain as day. Roy facing off with Bully. Like I was dreaming, it exploded into my mind's eye. The bull was readying for his charge, and the old man was stuck against the fence with no way out.

Bursting into a flat-out run, I careened out of the ruins and down the hill toward the farm. Leaping over the drywall, sheep scattered as I passed, bleating their annoyance as my feet pounded on the grass. Vaulting over another fence, I landed on the dirt road that led down to Roy's house and the pen where he kept the giant bull, creatively named Bully.

Rounding the house, I saw the top of the bull's back, but there was no sight of the old man anywhere. Bully lowered his head, the sound of his stamping hooves reaching my ears. It was then I realized I couldn't see Roy because he was already on the ground. *I couldn't be too late.*

"Boone!" Sean called out in a blind panic. "Stop!"

Spying Roy through the palings, I ignored Sean's cry and sprinted across the yard, but I wasn't fast enough. Bully's hoof came down hard on Roy's leg, and the old man bellowed in pain as the bone split. I heard the crack as plain as day, and I sprang into action.

It seemed I'd stopped thinking a long time ago and had allowed my senses to take over because I did the exact thing Roy—and Aileen for that matter—had warned me not to do. Run head first into danger without thinking.

Vaulting over the fence, I landed beside Roy and moved between him and Bully. My appearance startled the beast, and he moved backward, lowering his head and showing me his horns.

Bulls were stubborn creatures, highly temperamental and extremely dangerous if not handled correctly. Roy had taught me you had to show them who was the boss, or they would charge.

It was a constant struggle for dominance. I wasn't sure what'd happened, but Bully had decided he was king of the yard and skewered the old man.

I had to bluff my way through this or else Bully would trample us both. I'd heal given enough time, but Roy might never walk again.

"Boone, get out of here!" Roy cried.

Ignoring him, I held up my hands, never taking my gaze off Bully. The bull snorted, his eyes rolling, and stamped his forefoot on the ground.

"Whoa, Bully," I said soothingly.

The bull snorted again, his eyes rolling. I wasn't sure if it was my magic or the affinity I'd created when I first touched his hide all those weeks ago, but I could feel his anger. The air felt hot around him, much like the sensation that overcame me when Aileen used her powers.

Roy moaned behind me, struggling to drag himself through the mud to the gate. Bully's attention was drawn to the sound, and I whistled, bringing his eyes back to mine.

"Eyes on me, Bully," I said, edging to the side, drawing him away from Roy. The bull followed me, lowering his head and stamping on the ground. "That's it, you big pile of shite."

"Sweet mother of God," Sean exclaimed. "He's going to charge ye, Boone! Get outta there!"

Bully spooked at the sound of Sean's voice and

galloped forward. I had no idea what overcame me at that moment, but I leapt straight for him. One ton of pure muscle and a pair of menacing horns rushed toward me, and time slowed down.

My fingers hit metal, and I grasped the bullring through his nose. Tugging as hard as I could, I jerked Bully's head back down. He let out an angry bellow as I slipped under him, my head colliding with his chest and my legs almost trampled in the process.

Bully came to a halt, snorting and shaking his head, and my boots slipped on the churned mud as I righted myself. We were eye to eye this time, my grip on his bullring the only thing keeping him from bucking and ramming me in the chest.

"Sean," I said, still focused on the bull. "Get Roy out of here. *Now.*"

I was vaguely aware of the commotion behind me as I stared down the bull. He was looking right at me, his bulging eyes staring right into mine. I felt his anger and pain, the metal pulling on his nose to the point he was in agony, and I let go.

My hands slipped from the bullring, the pressure easing from Bully's snout, and before the bull had a chance to strike, I placed my hands on his head. Smack bang on the swirl of chestnut hair between his beady eyes.

My touch opened a pathway between us, and I

shook as images passed between us. His mind was empty, and all I could see was the blind rage that had taken over his base instincts of food, power, and mating. There was no way of deciphering what had set him off, but it didn't matter. He was angry, and when a bull was angry, he struck out. It was as simple as that.

"Calm, boy," I murmured.

Bully seemed to settle as I murmured to him, my fingers stroking his fur. After a minute, his eyes stopped rolling, and his breathing eased.

"Boone, we're out," Sean said from somewhere behind me. "Ye best follow."

Nodding, I was in complete agreement. The moment my palm left Bully's forehead, he retreated with a wild bellow, his hooves churning the mud and sending it flying. Taking the opportunity to get out of the pen while the going was good, I clambered over the fence out of harm's way.

Roy was lying on a patch of grass, his back resting against the bale of hay he must've been hauling in for Bully.

"What the hell was that?" Sean exclaimed, kneeling over him.

"He was on me before I knew what was happenin'," the old man replied, wincing. "I think me leg is broken. He stamped on me real good."

Sean glanced at me. "Boone, would ye wait here

while I run down to the house and call the ambulance? There's no movin' him without a great deal of trouble."

"Of course. Anything."

As Sean ran down the path, Roy glanced up at me, his frown created from more than pain.

"What did ye do to Bully, laddy?"

"I don't know," I murmured. "I really don't know."

As I sat there beside Roy waiting for the ambulance to arrive, I knew I'd used my power to calm Bully. There was no other explanation for it. He'd just backed down the moment my hands touched his fur, and that was that. How I'd done it was a complete mystery.

It wasn't until later that afternoon, I realized there was no possible way I could've heard Roy's cry for help inside the tower house. It could only mean my magic was growing.

I was finding my balance.

CHAPTER 9

"There Bully was, standin' over Roy, mad as a bee in a jar…"

Slouching in my seat, I wrapped my hand around my pint of beer and watched Sean McKinnon recount the story of my showdown with Bully. For what felt like the hundredth time in the last two weeks.

Molly McCreedy's was full of locals tonight, even Aileen had come, but it was all for a special occasion. Roy had come home from the hospital that morning, and this was his welcome home party. Any chance for little craic in this village.

The old man was sitting in the seat of honor beside the fireplace, a pint of ale in his hand, his cheeks red, a smile on his face, and his leg set on another chair before him. He'd been plastered from ankle to mid-thigh, and after an operation to put a metal pin in his femur, he had two weeks of recovery before he was allowed to return home. It seemed Bully had broken his leg in two, shattering the bone rather than snapping it. Hence, the metal rod.

"Boone leapt toward Bully with no fear at all," Sean declared, sweeping his arm wide. "He jumped..." He did the action, his boots thudding on the floorboards, the beer sloshing over the rim of the pint glass in his hand. "And grabbed Bully's bullring and swung off it like a trapeze artist."

"I can't believe you're still talking about that," I complained.

"Who lit the fuse on ye tampon, Boone?" Sean shot back. "You're the hero of the story. Ye should be thankin' me."

Hannah burst out into peals of laughter from behind the bar. "What happened next?"

"Yeah, Sean. What next?" someone called across the room.

"You all know what happened next," I said. "How many times have we heard this story?"

Sean held up his hand to shut me up and said, "Bully and Boone were eye to eye." He pointed to his eye and turned to show the room. "The air was thick with tension... Would Bully knock him flyin'? Or would he be the one to tame the wild beast?"

"*Ciach ort*," I swore in Irish.

"Let them have their fun," Aileen murmured beside me.

"I used my powers," I replied under my breath. "Blatantly."

"You didn't realize, and neither did they. They think you're the bull whisperer."

"You don't know how true that is."

"Oh, I can have a good guess," she replied.

I groaned and sipped on my beer. At least no more craglorn had been drawn to the village before or after the day Aileen had saved me by the hawthorn behind Sean's farmhouse.

"You did a good thing, Boone," she added. "Not only did you discover that your abilities as a shapeshifter run deeper, but you also saved a man's life. Bully could've trampled Roy to death, and this might've been a different kind of party."

I suppose she had a point. Time was a strange thing when you were stuck in the one place.

"Are you sure using my abilities won't draw any unwanted visitors?" I muttered under my breath.

"No, you're safe, Boone. What you do is instinctive. It's a part of your physiology. It's completely different to how a witch uses her magic."

"Then," Sean declared, the entire room hanging on his every word, "Boone let go. He let go of Bully's bullring. Can ye believe it? Standing a mere inch from an angry bull, *he let go*."

A dozen fists hit the table in a riotous exclamation. "No!" they chanted.

"Never fear! It wasn't over, not by a long shot. Boone placed his hands on Bully's head." He slapped his palm on Roy's forehead, much to the old man's amusement. "Then..." The room was on a knife's edge. "Then he sent Bully runnin' across the yard, his tail between his legs. Just like that!"

Everyone hollered and hooted, raising their glasses toward me. Embarrassed at the attention, I nodded, hiding behind the shock of unruly black curls that usually hung in my eyes. Lifting my pint, we drank, and with that, the story was over, and all eyes returned to Roy as he began recounting his stay in the hospital.

"Damn Bully shattered me leg, the *cúl tóna*," he was saying. "They cut me damn leg wide open and put metal rods inside. Can ye believe it?"

"Are you feeling better about everything?" Aileen asked now the attention was on Roy.

Setting my pint down, I inclined my head. "I guess so."

"Be a little more enthusiastic, Boone."

"All this chattering is exhausting," I said, nodding toward the room. "Ever since I touched

Bully's mind, the noise is hard to tune out. I never noticed it before."

"Then you must notice how Hannah looks at you." Aileen smirked and nodded toward the bar where the young woman was having a hard time keeping up with the demands of the villagers. "She's sweet on you."

Glancing over to the bar, I contemplated the notion of a romantic entanglement with a human woman. Hannah was pretty enough with her fiery hair and freckled cheeks, but I wasn't sure I could be with someone like that and not have them understand who I was. Keeping my abilities secret from Derrydun was hard enough, so what would happen when she wanted me to take her to Dublin for a weekend? Or even to the coast? I couldn't leave the boundary set by the hawthorns.

I must've been staring at her too long because she turned and saw my gaze was fixed on her. She caught my eye, her cheeks flushed slightly, and winked.

"I know," I said to Aileen. "I can feel it, and not in an inappropriate way."

She laughed softly. "I was about to say... With that and your bare ass, I've had about enough of you."

"You're like my mam if I do say so," I retorted, not even missing a beat.

"You're making me feel old. I'd stop it if I were you."

I thought about her daughter Skye and smiled. I wasn't too old that I could be her son, and honestly, our relationship was more than a witch helping a shapeshifter. In the few short months I'd been in Derrydun, she'd become just that. A surrogate mother with all the trimmings.

Finishing her lemonade, the witch turned to me. "I'm off for the evening."

"Aye, I'm not far behind you."

"Don't leave on my account. You should flirt a little with Hannah. Have some fun. Wouldn't hurt, you know."

"I've had just about enough excitement for one evening," I replied, not wanting to lead Hannah on. "I might go for a run to clear my head."

"Don't forget to give your best to Roy before you do," Aileen commanded in her motherly way. "After the mess with Bully, he thinks of you as a son."

"I know…"

"I'm sure you do," she said mysteriously before rising to her feet and smoothing down her skirt.

Taking her cue, I approached the old man and smiled.

"Ah, Boone," Roy declared, patting the chair next to him. "Have a seat and chat with me."

Sitting beside him, I studied his cast. Someone

had put a brightly colored hand-woven sock over his foot.

"I missed ye at the hospital," he said.

"I know you don't like to be fawned over, so I helped Sean make sure things were running on the farm. But after tonight, I'm not so sure about that."

"I must say, I'm likin' the rise in popularity."

Smiling, I looked around the room, and all I could feel was warmth. It was rather nice. These people genuinely cared about one another, no matter how many shades of crazy they were. Even old Fergus—the ancient Irishman who sat out near the coach bay every day with his donkey and scrappy little dog, selling his hand-woven crosses of St. Brigid to tourists—had come in for a drink. The donkey had to stay outside, but his dog sat by his chair as quiet as a mouse.

"How did ye do it?" Roy asked. "How did ye calm Bully like ye did?"

"I can't say," I replied with a shrug. "I knew I had to distract him long enough for Sean to drag you out so...I distracted him."

"That was more than distractin'," Roy stated. "I've never seen a man stand eye to eye with a bull like that in me life. Sixty years of farmin' and handlin' bulls and never..."

"I wish I knew."

Roy eyed me with an air of skepticism.

"Sometimes, I'm not sure how to take ye, lad."

"What do you mean?" I didn't like the sound of that, and my skin bristled as I felt wariness fill the air around him.

"Ye don't talk about your past much, do ye?"

I frowned. "There's not much in it. Derrydun is my home now, and everything before is irrelevant."

"Ye don't have the Guard after ye? Last thing anyone needs, especially Aileen, is the law comin' down on her."

I shook my head and laughed. "Take it easy, Roy," I said, rising to my feet. "Don't you worry about the farm. I'll be there with Sean in the morning. You can count on that."

"Ye little bugger," he cursed after me.

Outside, the air was clear, and I shook off the warmth that had overtaken Molly McCreedy's. Fergus's donkey raised her head from the cast-iron pot at her feet and immediately disregarded me, sticking her nose back into the chaff.

"Nice to see you too, girl," I murmured, placing my palm on her back. Immediately, I felt her sense of satisfaction. That must be some good chaff.

"You going home already?"

Glancing into the darkness, I caught sight of Hannah leaning against the side of the pub.

"Aye, I'm not big on all the attention."

"I can tell." She pushed off the wall and came to

stand before me. "You're a bit of a mystery, aren't you?"

"There's not much to me," I replied.

"Tall, dark, handsome, and brooding..." She edged closer, placing her hands on my shoulders. "That's very sexy, you know."

Her palms wrapped around my neck, her fingers teasing the hair at my nape. It felt good to have a woman touch me, and as her lips moved closer, I knew this wasn't right. I couldn't give her romance or a relationship or a family...not even a little bit of fun. I had too many secrets, and they would forever keep me apart from those things. The *more* kind of things.

I wrapped my hands around her wrists and moved my head back. "Hannah..."

"Shite," she cursed, letting me go. "I misread everything, didn't I?"

"You're pretty and all but... I can't. I'm sorry."

Embarrassment mixed with disappointment bled from her skin, and she turned her face from mine.

"I don't want to lead you on, Hannah," I went on, not wanting to upset her. "It's not right."

"You're a rare man, Boone," she said, shaking her head. "One day, someone will catch you, and the rest of us will die of jealousy. You'll see."

I hoped she was right because I wasn't sure how long I would be satisfied with living a life among everyone but being apart at the same time. Eventually, something had to break.

As Hannah walked back into Molly McCreedy's, the donkey raised her head and let out an enthusiastic *hee-haw*.

CHAPTER 10

And so life in Derrydun went on much the same way as it always did.

Autumn faded into winter, and snow covered the far-off mountains, and the very tip of Croagh Patrick was ice. Then the melt came, and the weather bloomed into spring. Flowers erupted, and the landscape burst with color. Lush emerald ferns coated the ground while wild fuchsia tinted it with shades of cherry and plum.

Animals came out of hibernation, and young ones were born left, right, and center. I could feel the ebb of life in the air, my powers growing sharper than the edge of a carving knife. The farm was alive with it as the herd welcomed lamb after lamb and three calves fathered by the troublesome Bully to the fold.

It was a peaceful time. A good time. But with all

things, the lure of growth and bounty drew greedy eyes and unwanted attention.

One morning, in early spring, I was on my rounds of the farm. The air was crisp, signaling any kind of true warmth was a long way off yet, and a fine layer of dew coated the ground. Droplets of water sparkled in the sunrise, and light forced its way through the fog, limiting my line of sight. Ahead, I could see the fine outline of a group of sheep huddled together, but further afield, the mist clung into the dips and valleys of the landscape. I would wager that not five meters above my head, the air was free and clear.

It was a beautiful sight, but I still buried deeper into my coat to stave off the chill.

My boots squished on the wet grass, the toes damp with dew as I crossed the top field, counting sheep and checking the drywalls. It was the time of year lambs popped out without warning, so we had to make sure the little ones that might've been born during the night were well, along with their mams. Predators roamed the land and the sky, waiting for unsuspecting babes to be forgotten by their mothers long enough for them to be snatched. It was my job to make sure none of that happened and if it did, deal with the horrible aftermath.

My nose twitched as a foreign scent flitted past, and I raised my head. Raking my gaze over the field, it took a moment before I noticed the fox sitting by the gate. Hidden by the mist, its russet fur blended into the landscape, its snout twitching slightly as it scented me in return. It was so still, it was no wonder I hadn't noticed it until the wind changed. Breathing in again, I noted it was a female.

The fox stared directly at me, and I reached out with my power, intending to frighten her away, but there was nothing for it to grasp onto. There was no emotion or even any base instinct emitting from the animal. It was strange, and the lack of anything tangible for me to find raised a mighty large red flag. Frowning, I waited...and so did the fox.

Leaning against the drywall, I glanced at the sheep and the lambs frolicking at their mother's feet. If she were here to snatch a newborn, she would regret it while I was on the lookout. I considered shifting into my fox form to scare her away, but I quickly disregarded the idea. Aileen had instilled in me the virtue of patience and care, especially where using my abilities so blatantly were concerned. There were still many things out there I didn't understand about the world of magic, so I had to be careful.

What had Aileen told me about the fae of the forests? They were tricksters, shades, and phantoms...though not all were troublesome. The fox could be any one of those or something darker with a taste for malicious behavior. Like the craglorn, it could be an illusion designed to lure me from the protection of the hawthorns and into the clutches of whoever had stolen my memories.

The doorway to the fae realm had been sealed long ago, but there was every likelihood that some of those spirits still roamed the forests even after all this time. Desperate for magic, the friendly fairies of the forests could've twisted into something evil.

Or the fox could be another shapeshifter...just like me.

I wasn't sure why the thought alarmed me. Perhaps it had everything to do with the wolves and the ravens that had been attempting to chase me down the first night I began remembering. Or perhaps it was the lack of power I felt from the creature. I could sense Aileen's magic, and the craglorn had sensed mine when I was in animal form, so wouldn't that mean I would be able to feel out another shapeshifter when I saw one? I wasn't entirely sure.

Watching the fox closely, I noticed she didn't even pay a scrap of attention to the lambs. If she wasn't hungry, then why was she here?

Ignoring the niggling sensation in the back of my mind that was warning me she was here for me, I pushed off the fence and walked toward the group of sheep, keeping my body between them and the fox. I approached, placing my heel down before my toe to quieten my footsteps, and counted six of Roy's blue and three of Mark Ashlyn's orange from over the rise. He was an English fellow, who'd moved to Ireland for love when he was a young man.

Counting three lambs, I waited until they suckled before I gave them a dab of paint on their asses to claim ownership. One blue and two orange.

After a while, I glanced over my shoulder to check on the fox, but she'd disappeared. Snorting, I watched the sheep graze their way across the top of the field. She must've given up on whatever reason she'd come here for. Whatever it was.

For three days, the fox returned, and each time, she sat and stared, neither approaching or moving away.

I never saw her arrive, and I never saw her leave. She never approached the herd, me, or attempted to snatch a vulnerable lamb. Her strange behavior led me to believe she was something more than a mere fox, but there was no way for me to tell without revealing myself...but one thing was crystal clear.

She was there for me.

We were both aware of the other, our silent exchange speaking louder than any words. She wanted me to follow, and I wasn't willing. Then she would appear the next day, and we'd do it all over again.

On the fourth morning, I'd had enough. She sat in her usual position, waiting, but this time, I stared into her eyes and shook my head. Wherever she wanted to lead me, I wasn't going. I had a duty to Aileen and Derrydun. This time, unlike my insatiable curiosity when it came to the hawthorn by Sean's house, I would think before I leapt into the unknown.

Then, to my utter surprise, the fox rose and flipped her tail before turning and walking away. Her paws were silent on the earth, her form melting into the mists like an apparition. It was like she'd never been there at all.

Grimacing, I returned to my duties, confident I'd made the right decision by ignoring the fox's silent request.

CHAPTER 11

I didn't know why I kept the encounter with the fox from Aileen, but the animal didn't return, and the early morning meetings slipped from my mind.

Life settled once more, and I began to explore my powers, testing the limits of my imagination. So far, I'd learned I had an empathy with animals and people, the ability to sense their emotions was rather annoying at times, but it had come in handy, especially after the encounter with Bully.

Then there was my instinctive nature when it came to sensing magic and the use of it. I could also change into multiple forms but had not yet attempted anything other than the fox and gyrfalcon I was used to. If my ability extended to other shapes, I wasn't entirely sure. I'd yet to try, afraid I'd become stuck halfway.

Walking the drywall by Mark Ashlyn's place, I was greeted by the black stallion that prowled the outer edges of the neighboring property. His proud head emerged from the mist, vapor billowing from his nostrils. Beyond, I could barely make out the outline of the three mares—two chestnuts and a cream and chestnut Appaloosa—grazing along the hillside.

"Top of the morning, Knight," I murmured as the stallion lowered his head over the drywall. A wire fence had been erected along this stretch to keep the horses from leaping in with the sheep, but there was still enough room for him to lean over and nuzzle my hand.

As I stroked his fur, my mind touched his, and the sensation of greeting a familiar animal warmed my insides. During the time I'd worked on Roy's farm, I'd come to know all the animals that lived on the hillside, from the sheep, the horses, the cows, and the birds that wheeled overhead to the badgers and hares that leapt through the forest. Even the occasional group of red deer would be sighted, protected closely by a grand stag with antlers that twisted toward the sky.

Threading my fingers through Knight's mane, I wondered if I would be able to manage taking on his form. We were great friends these days, our morning ritual of chatting over the fence had brought us closer together, and I knew the stallion inside out.

What would it feel like to become Knight? I imagined a stallion would be powerful, proud, and regal...but what would it feel like as a shapeshifter?

Deciding to take the risk, I stroked Knight's velvety nose and stepped back.

"No time like the present," I said to him. "You had better ready yourself, boy. This is going to be totally weird."

Focusing on the stallion, my flesh began to heat, and sweat beaded on my forehead as I began changing. Then my bones stretched, signaling the point of no return. Grimacing, I fell to my knees as everything snapped and twisted, morphing from a human physiology into that of the black stallion.

Knight snorted, stamping his hoof. His eyes bulged, and he whinnied before trotting off toward the mares, leaving me to change into his likeness.

My arms lengthened into legs, my hips twisted into a strong rump, a tail sprouted at the base of my spine, and my face elongated. Black fur grew all over my body as my clothes dropped to the ground, and before long, I stood tall and proud, the spitting image of Knight.

Realizing I'd done what I thought was impossible, I leaped and bucked with glee, galloping across the top field like a maniac, relishing the power coiled in my body. Slowing to a trot, I shook my head, snorting. *What a rush.*

Knowing I didn't have much time before Roy expected me down at the farmhouse, I willed my body to change back. I could endure the pain that came with my transformations much better after months of practice channeling the energy back into my limbs. By the time I was a man again, I was calm and collected, no signs that the snapping of bones and the twisting of muscle and sinew had ever ravaged me at all.

Kneeling in the grass, butt naked yet again, I smiled at Knight and his brood. The stallion lowered his head and snorted, vapor billowing from his nostrils in a silent show of approval. It seemed he liked me as a horse.

What a rush, indeed.

The following day, I found Aileen at Irish Moon, sitting behind the counter with her tarot cards in hand.

It was her morning ritual, and like clockwork, she sat in that exact place and divined her daily messages. Then the buses would start coming, and there would be a constant stream of tourists going to and fro from the shops until late afternoon. She never needed my help, but I came when I had a spare moment between all of my part-time jobs.

"I made a new shape," I said proudly, leaning on the counter.

She raised her eyebrows. "Is that so? Did you get tired of foxes and falcons?"

"You always say I should learn to hone my abilities. I honed."

"Then what shape did you make? I can see you're itching to tell someone about it."

"A horse," I said proudly.

Aileen smirked. "Be careful, or people will think a kelpie has come to drag them away."

Smiling, I shook my head. The kelpie was an ancient Irish horse that rose from the ocean and dragged unsuspecting folk into the water so it could drown them.

"It wasn't as difficult as I thought," I went on. "I've been greeting Mark Ashlyn's horses every time I venture toward his property. It didn't take long to form an affinity with them."

"Imagine you," Aileen said with a chuckle. "Prancing about like a pony."

I laughed at her jibe and rogue, "I'm not sure I like it, though. I never realized how fragile a horse's legs felt."

"Aye, they seem to break easily, that's for sure,

but I know little about them, to be honest. Have you tried any other shapes?"

"There's Father O'Donegal's tabby cat," I said with a wink. "But I fear you would be making fun of me until the end of time."

She smiled weakly and returned her gaze to the cards. It was far from the reaction I was expecting to my lighthearted joke, and I began to worry.

"Are you all right?" I asked, sitting beside her. "You don't seem yourself this morning. Are you feeling sick?"

Aileen waved me off. "I'm fine. The cards are giving me grief this morning, is all."

Glancing at the counter, I saw the card she'd been meditating on when I'd walked in. The Tower sat before her, and I frowned.

"Something keeps warning me," she muttered, the lightness of our conversation taking a dark turn. "It's been this way for months. More than a year, now I think of it. How long have you been with me?"

"A year, all told."

Her fingers traced over the gold outline on the card. "Then longer still..."

"But things have been well," I said. "Only what happened at the hawthorn." I winced at the memory, the phantom claws of the craglorn pinching around my waist. "Nothing came..."

"No, but other things can. Life isn't a long line

of contentment, Boone. It rises and falls like the tides in the ocean. Good comes with bad, and bad comes with good. There can't be one without the other."

"You fear something is coming?"

"I've seen it in the cards time and time again," she replied. "I only worry that it's not come."

"You and your precious cards," I said, rolling my eyes. "Could it be that not everything is tied to them? The future is not set in stone, after all. You taught me that."

"You're right, but there's something different about this. The frequency can't be explained by chance. There's a force in play here..."

"If there were other magic in Derrydun, you would know it," I stated.

"Every time I divine my daughter's future, I draw The Tower," she went on, ignoring me. "Without fail."

I didn't understand. All this time she'd been divining Skye's future, not her own? I'd always believed she'd been meditating on her duty to protect Derrydun from magical threats, not a woman who lived on the other side of the world. Her daughter...

"Why do you think that is?" I asked, not pressing.

Aileen picked up the card and studied it intently. "The Tower must fall in order to be rebuilt."

"That doesn't sound so bad," I replied. "Maybe it means she's starting out on a new path."

"Or picking up where someone left off..."

"You said it yourself," I declared, attempting to reassure her. "You haven't seen her since she was a few years old. It could mean a thousand different things. It's not a bad card, remember?"

The witch was silent for a moment, her gaze angled away from mine. I imagined I could feel the delicate ebb of her magic, but it was gone before I could sense it out.

"Enough about that," Aileen said, returning the card to the deck and shuffling. "Let's draw one for you."

"Another?"

"Why not? Humor me."

Sensing her apathy, I nodded. "Go ahead."

She shuffled the deck vigorously, then placed it facedown on the counter. Sweeping the cards out in a long fan, she gestured for me to pick. My palm hovered over the black rectangles, and when I felt the familiar pull of energy, I selected one closer to me.

I was never sure if it was my mind playing tricks or if there was magic in the tarot legacy calling to my own, but I always felt something when Aileen asked me to draw. Every time.

Turning the card over, I saw it was another image

from the Major Arcana. The twenty-two cards—twenty-three counting The Fool—that represented the major archetypes of the human consciousness. By now, I knew a lesson was coming, and it would either annoy or help me.

"The Magician," Aileen declared.

"Sounds fancy."

"Be careful, Boone," she said mysteriously. "The Magician is all about illusion, after all. He may be a beneficent guide, but he doesn't always have our best interests at heart."

"Why are these cards always full of ominous warnings?" I grumbled.

"Life is a gamble," the witch said with a shrug. "There's always room for a little warning, especially for us."

"If you say so. What warning should I heed this time?"

She held up the card so I could see it. "A manipulator may be in play, or it may be your ego that's doing the manipulating. Be careful your power doesn't intoxicate you...for good or bad."

Instantly, I thought about the fox. A manipulator and a magician fond of illusions. Even more of a reason to believe I'd made the right decision.

"So I better be careful adding to my menagerie," I said. "Noted."

"Better hold back on the house cat for a while."

She smiled weakly and returned the card to the deck. I got the distinct impression something was bothering her, and it wasn't entirely to do with The Tower.

"I'm worried about you, Aileen," I said, watching her pack away the deck. "The cards have you rattled."

"Never you mind about me," she replied. "I can deal with the messages the cards have thrown at me. I've been doing it for almost thirty years."

"I don't doubt it, but..."

She turned to face me, cocking her eyebrow. "But?"

"There's something bothering you... Something more than the cards."

She was silent, her eyes drilling into mine like she was using her magic to read my intentions. I wouldn't be surprised if she was.

"I can help you protect Derrydun," I went on. "I'm ready."

"Perhaps you're right," she said carefully.

Warmth tickled my skin, and the awareness of magic pulled at the edges of my being. Aileen's smiled faded, and I knew it wasn't coming from her.

"Aileen?" I asked as the temperature grew.

"*Shh,*" she said, holding up her hand. Her expression took on a dreamy state, and her eyes appeared to focus on something far away.

Warmth turned into a prickling sensation, my skin zapping as if it were charged with static electricity. The tingling flowed through my entire body, and for a moment, I almost believed I was about to change against my will, but the feeling ceased as abruptly as it began. Focusing my mind, I was pulled toward the west side of the village... toward the hawthorn where I'd encountered the craglorn.

My heart sank, and I knew...

"The hawthorn..." I began uneasily.

Aileen sighed and didn't move. Not even an inch.

"You're not going to do anything?" I asked, turning to look in the direction of the tree.

Aileen shook her head. "There's nothing to be done. It's gone."

Then as soon as it had begun, the tingling ceased, and it was like it had never been there at all. With one last burst of magic, the hawthorn had died.

"I had a delivery last night," Aileen said. "Would you help me unpack it?"

"*Aileen*," I said with irritation.

The witch turned and glared at me. "Boone, listen to me. The hawthorn has died, and that is that. There is no saving or replacing it. It's gone. Life goes on. It must."

The tree was gone, and with it, my world had

shrunk by a third. All the more reason to protect Derrydun and its two remaining hawthorns.

"But—"

"You either have to stay within the boundary of what remains or gather the courage to face what's waiting on the other side," Aileen said, preempting my complaint. "It's that simple."

My expression fell, and the excitement I'd felt that morning seemed to have come from a lifetime I hardly remembered. Leave Derrydun? I wasn't sure it was an option. Anyone and anything could be out there waiting, and who knew what they would do to me if I were caught.

Aileen placed her hand on my arm. "When you're ready, you'll know what to do."

CHAPTER 12

There was nothing I could do about the hawthorn and the loss of its protection, so like Aileen, I went on with life as usual.

It was what it was. My world had shrunk, and short of planting a new tree, I was trapped as I'd always been. One day, I would cross the border and find what, or who, was waiting for me, but I wasn't ready for that confrontation.

Closing up the kitchen at Molly McCreedy's for the night, I ventured out into the pub to find Sean in the same place I'd left him a half hour ago. It had worn on close to midnight, and the farmer was still here, his ass welded to his favorite barstool. I'd lost count of how many times I'd escorted him home, but I still humored him.

"You still here?" I asked, leaning against the bar.

"Still tryin' to get another beer," he grumbled,

"but Hannah won't serve me anymore." He pouted at her and declared, "I thought we had somethin'."

"We've never had anything," she said, not even glancing up from the last of her cleaning duties. "You're past the point of drunk, and it's my call. Besides, it's closing, and I want to go home."

"You're no fun, Hannah," Sean complained. "One more! *Just one.*"

"You've been having 'just one more' all night," she said, waggling her finger at the farmer. "Off with you, Sean McKinnon, before I hose you out the door."

"She'll do it, you know," I said with a chuckle.

"And what are ye still doin' here?" he complained. "Kitchen closed an hour ago."

"What kind of man would I be if I left Hannah here to close up on her lonesome with a fool like you crowing for just one more beer?" I winked and laughed as he shoved my shoulder.

"You're too smart for ye own good," he said trying to hide his own smile. "Ahh, I best be off."

"You'll make it, I trust?" I asked him, and he flipped me his middle finger before shuffling out into the night. I suppose his answer was a resounding yes.

"Thanks for that," Hannah said as the door swung shut with a bang.

"He's harmless," I replied. "He just needs a little encouragement."

"I know. It's just wearing thin, is all."

"He'll come to terms with it one day," I muttered. "It's coming up to three years since his wife passed."

"Exactly."

"Hannah," I scolded her.

"Sorry, sorry," she muttered, reaching behind the bar and retrieving her bag. "I know I should be kinder, but the man's a borderline alcoholic. I worry."

"It's difficult, that's for sure," I mused, thinking of the friendship Sean and I had. "But we look out for one another in Derrydun. He loved her more than we could ever understand. I never met her, but it's not hard to tell how he felt. That kind of loss must cut deep. I can't begin to wonder what it feels like. Cut him some slack, all right? I'll watch out for him."

We crossed the pub, and I flicked off the lights as we went. Outside, Hannah fumbled in her bag for the keys as I waited. The only light came from the orange streetlamps, and in the distance, the green glow from the single set of traffic lights. The street was empty, and all the shops were dark, but I knew strange and wonderful things still lingered out there, and not everyone was aware of the eyes that watched.

"You're a wise man. Anyone ever tell you that?"

Hannah declared, turning the key in the lock. The mechanism clicked, and she glanced at me, raising an eyebrow.

I snorted and rolled my eyes. "I'm more like an animal behaviorist than a wise man."

Hannah laughed, her face lighting up. "And our Sean is a rare animal indeed."

"Careful," I said playfully.

"Would you walk with me?" she asked, nodding toward the forest. "It's so pretty on a night like this, and I know you like to wander there, too."

I frowned, not realizing she knew I ventured into the wilderness at all hours past midnight.

Hannah laughed again. "C'mon, Boone. It's a small village. People talk...and they see more than you might realize."

Hesitating, I began to fret she'd seen me walk into the trees as a man and fly out as a gyrfalcon. Or worse still, seen me change, bare ass and all.

She raised an eyebrow. "You're not hiding any dead bodies out there are you? Is that why you left wherever it was you came from to live here? The Guard was getting too close to finding out you were a serial killer?"

Her lips quirked, signaling she was taking the piss, and I rolled my eyes. "Hardly."

"Then let's walk. Since you're not an axe murderer, what harm could it do?"

Sighing, I lowered my head, my hair falling into my eyes. "Lead the way, then."

She smiled brightly and nodded toward the path that ran between Molly McCreedy's and the handcrafts store next door.

The track ran behind the shops, along the side of the stream that ran through the parkland by the coach bay, past the church and its ancient graveyard, and then into a stretch of the forest I'd become familiar with in my nighttime wanderings as a fox.

The hawthorn that sat in the middle of the road protected this part of the village, and the air felt cooler as a result. The safety net was thinner here, so it was a place I didn't venture to often. Still, I wasn't worried walking the path with Hannah. I knew she lived a little further along and well within the limits of where I was able to wander.

We followed the stream for a while, the bubbling water calming in the silence. Our feet crunched on the earth below, the scent of the wilderness floating all around. The damp smells of dirt, the sweetness of the fuchsia, and the crispness of the unpolluted air... it was beautiful. I felt at home among all of it. To nature, I was insignificant, its ancient power eclipsing anything I'd ever been or would be. I was a blip on its surface while it would go on living long after my bones rotted away.

Stepping out into a glade, silver light poured

over us, and I turned my face upward.

"Oh, the stars are so pretty," Hannah said breathlessly, her face tilted up toward the sky. "Don't you think, Boone?"

I peered at the thousands of tiny silver pricks of light and nodded. "Aye. To be sure."

Signaling she was far from done with me and her evening walk, she sat gracefully in the middle of the glade, her eyes trained upward. Reluctantly, I sat beside her, respectfully keeping my distance. This was becoming more and more like a romantic date, and it put me on edge. Hannah was lovely, but...

"Why don't you talk about where you were before?" she asked abruptly. "Was it that bad?"

"It's not worth mentioning," I replied with a shrug. "It doesn't seem to matter all that much anymore."

She tilted her head to the side, her fiery curls brushing against her cheek. "What about your family? They don't matter?"

"Honestly, I don't remember them."

"Really?" She frowned, her eyebrows knitting together. "It's been a long time since I've seen mine, but I remember everything about them."

"Why haven't you seen them?" I asked, turning her questioning around.

"Distance, mainly. It's not that I don't want to, but sometimes, circumstances just make it impossible."

"I'm sorry. It sounds like you miss them."

Hannah shrugged, glancing back up at the stars. "A rock and a hard place... What can you do? Sometimes, things are the way they are just because it's the way they turned out."

I could relate to that in more ways than she would ever realize.

"Boone..."

I turned to face her, the uncertainty in her voice unsettling.

"There's really no chance for us?" she asked, lowering her gaze. "I'd very much like to... Well, you know."

"Hannah..." Bowing my head, I grimaced. "I just... You're beautiful and sweet... I just don't see you that way."

Silence stretched between us, and I fidgeted nervously, pulling at the grass by my feet. If I were cruel, I would lead her on and take the comfort she offered for a night or two, but I wasn't like that. Breaking her heart was never something that would appeal. It wasn't in me to take when I wasn't able to give.

"I think it's time to reveal myself to you," she mused, standing before me.

Perplexed, I watched as she began unbuttoning her blouse. *Oh, no.* When she said reveal, she meant...

"Hannah, what are you doing? I can't..."

She smiled and allowed her blouse to fall to the forest floor. Then her bra followed, and her skirt, and the rest of her underthings.

"Hannah, I think you shouldn't—"

"*Shhh*," she murmured. "You'll see soon enough."

All at once, I sensed magic in the air, and then there was the sound of snapping bones as she began to shrink and sprout red fur.

I rose to my feet, my eyes wide with shock. She was *changing* and not into just any creature. She was changing into a *fox*.

"You're the fox from the field," I said, shaking my head. "You were the one who came..."

"Come," she said, her voice husky as her face elongated, her nose turned black, and her freckled cheeks sprouted whiskers. "Come and see..."

For a long time, I stood and watched her. She'd completed her transformation and contentedly sat and waited for me to make up my mind. I wasn't surprised considering she'd tried for four days to get my attention.

Weighing up my options, I knew there were two ways this could go. I could find a companion in Hannah as a shapeshifter, or she could be leading me to my doom. The doom part sounded rather bad, but the temptation of not hiding my true nature was more alluring than anything I'd ever felt.

Loneliness was something I'd struggled with since learning I had to keep my magic a secret, and belonging was all I'd ever wanted. There were others out there like me, but I was alone in my plight. Aileen was a witch, and we had that connection, but as a shapeshifter, I had no one.

I was a part of Derrydun, but I was still separate.

If Hannah was revealing herself to me, then with her, I might have a chance at being understood. Besides, she might know others like us and had been attempting to lead me to them all this time. More importantly, she might have the answers I'd been searching for since my new life began. *Who was I?*

That was why I began to change. Call it a leap of faith, but I had to know one way or another. The call in my blood was too strong not to.

Hannah didn't make a sound as I transformed, waiting patiently as my flesh and bones snapped, twisted, and reformed into the first shape I'd ever been. The fox. *Running...*

I sat on my haunches and licked my paws, easing into the last intricacies of my fox shape. When I was done, I glanced at Hannah and bowed my head. I was ready.

Turning, she trotted off through the forest, leading me toward an unknown destination, and this time...I followed.

CHAPTER 13

The darkness came alive with shade and depth when I was in my fox form.

My eyesight was sharper, my hearing attuned to the undercurrents of nature, and my sense of smell was heightened. Ahead, I could see the outline of Hannah's fox form as she led me through the forest. Her tail hung low, and her footsteps were lithe as she leapt over fallen logs and weaved through trees, taking me to an unknown destination.

Whatever she wanted to show me was still a mystery, but she'd become desperate enough to reveal her true form in order to get me there.

The closer we ventured toward the edges of my known world, the more uneasy I became. I wanted to trust Hannah, but her reluctance to confide had me on edge. Was she the sweet barmaid I'd always known, or was she something more sinister?

I felt the boundary of the hawthorns before me, and I stopped, my snout brushing up against the invisible veil. I could feel the hum of magic before me, and beyond that, nothing. One more step and I would be exposed.

Hannah sensed my uneasiness and turned, her gaze meeting mine. Seeing I'd halted, she sat on her haunches and waited for me to make my decision.

Before me, there was untold danger, but there were also answers. Behind, there was Derrydun and safety. Did I want to know the truth of who I was badly enough to brush with death? I'd come to terms with the life I led now. I was Boone, but it was only a small part of who I was...of who I'd been.

That was why I stepped across the boundary.

Hannah led me on, weaving her way through parts of the countryside I was unfamiliar with. The air seemed colder outside the influence of the hawthorns, but in the distance, I could feel the presence of another. It seemed there were many places of sanctuary for me across Ireland, and I was grateful to know it.

Finally, we came to a halt in the middle of a clearing. Above, the stars shone through the bows that hung overhead, their leaves rustling in the breeze. There was nothing here, and I wondered what she would gain from bringing me to this place.

Hannah stopped, sniffed the air, and began to

change. It was strange to watch another shapeshifter morph into a human form. The elongating of her limbs, the shedding of her fur, the growth of her russet-colored hair... I wondered if I looked just as strange. Not wanting to dwell on it, I initiated my own transformation, turning my back to give her some semblance of modesty.

"I knew you would come," Hannah said behind me as I stood on two feet once more.

Turning, I met her gaze. She stood across the clearing, naked and shimmering, her hair wild and fluttering around her delicate face as if she were alight with an unearthly fire. There was something about her that didn't quite make sense, and my head began to throb the harder I tried to unravel the mystery.

"You're a shapeshifter?" I asked, attempting to keep my gaze from falling to her nakedness. "Like me?"

"I can change my shape, but I'm nothing like you," she replied, her lips curving into a wicked smile as her eyes raked greedily over my body. It seemed she liked what she saw.

"Then what are you?"

She prowled across the clearing, her feet making no sound on the litter on the forest floor, and stood before me. Without uttering a word, she placed her palms on my chest and caressed my skin, her teeth tugging at her bottom lip.

"Hannah..." I murmured.

"You're no fun," she complained, letting her head fall back. "She said you were the most cunning...and loyal."

"Who?" I asked, grasping her wrists. "Who said that to you?"

"You should at least kiss me once," she said. "Pretty boy Boone, with your handsome pouty lips. Imagine what they could do...*down there*."

"Who are you?" I growled, shaking her.

Hannah's fiery curls shook back and forth, and she began to giggle hysterically.

"They really gave you the works," she chortled. "I'm a fae, you dolt. I can't believe you didn't recognize me, but I suppose that was the point."

My eyes widened, and my grasp slackened on her wrists. She wriggled free and slid her body against mine, taking the opportunity to borderline molest me.

"Who are you to me?" I asked, attempting to extract myself from her wandering hands.

"I'm Hannah," she replied. "I could be *your* Hannah...if you want. There's still time to go back."

"Hannah," I said, becoming rather uncomfortable. "Why did you bring me here?"

"The hawthorn is gone," she said. "I needed it to

survive. It's too risky to feed off the tree in the village, and it would be a death sentence to even approach the ancient hawthorn in the forest behind the tower house. Aileen would skin me alive, she would, but if I were yours, then I could stay."

Could it be that Aileen didn't know a fae had been living under her nose? I'd spoken to Hannah many times at Molly McCreedy's and had never sensed anything magical about her. Not once.

"You're not making any sense..."

"Without the tree, I had to do something," she went on, her fingers tracing over my face. "I'm sorry, Boone, but I was desperate. It is life or death for me, you know. I've waited a long time for someone like you, but I've waited for a chance to go home longer." She mewled softly, then kissed me on the lips. "We could've had a great deal of fun, you know. Flying, running, making love in whatever form you wanted. I was up for anything..."

I shoved her away with a growl. "What have you done?"

Hannah pouted. "I think the question is what have you done, Boone?"

"Me?" I couldn't remember a single thing from my past. My first memory was of fear and running. I'd always believed I was the victim, but what if I was the bad guy? What if I was running from my punishment? What if I'd done something terrible?

"She wants you."

"Who?" I exclaimed, my patience wearing thin. "Who wants me?"

"Carman is coming, and there's no stopping her," Hannah said. "She will reign over this realm and open the doorways. This world of technology and humanity...*gone*."

Carman... She was the thousand-year-old witch Aileen had told me about. The witch who'd betrayed her kind and who had been banished from ever returning to Ireland. What did she want from me? Was it just my magic she wanted to suck from my bones, or was she the force I'd been fleeing the night I landed in Derrydun?

"The doorways... Is that the only reason witches are being hunted for their magic?" I asked. "What have I got to do with a world I don't belong to?"

Hannah's playful expression crumpled into pure anger. "The doorways should never have been closed! I've been stuck in a thousand different lives, watching and waiting for my way home to open. But it never does... You know what it's like to be trapped. *You know*."

Growling, I strode forward and grasped her around the neck, my fingers digging into her throat. I was tired of her games, her trickery. I needed answers like I needed air to breathe. Hannah had lured me here to be caught by Carman, and I had no idea why I deserved to die—if I was to die at all. There was no way I was going down without a fight.

"Who am I?" I shouted at the fae. "*Who am I?*"

A searing burst of magic erupted from her, and her body began to change. Her soft pallor morphed into the rough texture of bark and wood, her eyes shining emerald and her hair threading into long twisting vines. Opening her mouth, a primal cry burst from between her lips, and branches exploded out of her back.

I let her go, stumbling backward in surprise at her sudden transformation. Her mind reached out and thrust into mine, cutting deep as she sank her claws into me.

Falling to my knees, I roared in pain as branches whipped around me, throwing me across the clearing. My back hit the trunk of an ancient oak, my head cracking painfully. Before I could move, shards of wood pierced my flesh, slicing through both arms and legs, pinning me in place.

My entire body shuddered, and my bones snapped...but they didn't reform. My limbs dangled uselessly, blood oozing from the wounds Hannah had inflicted. Everything was pain and fire. Fire and pain.

"Don't try that again," she said angrily, her voice vibrating through my veins and into my soul. "You can't change, Boone, I won't allow it."

Raising my head, I saw her clearly for the first time. She stood tall, her entire body resembling an ancient tree, her body covered in bark and moss, her hair tangled ivy, and her eyes...they glowed iridescent green in the darkness. Several branches had erupted from her back and stabbed through my flesh, growing so fast it was impossible to get out of the way.

A hazy memory nudged the edges of my mind. Her kind didn't live on the shores of Ireland, but a lot of things had changed in the last thousand years. What was she? I sifted through the haze, trying to find the name of her true form, for that was what stood before me. Her true skin.

"Spriggan," I whispered. "Trickster, shapeshifter, fae of the forest..."

"So you do remember me," she said with interest.

"Hannah..." I moaned. "Don't do this. Do you think she cares about you?" I had no idea what Carman wanted with my magic or me, but I had no other recourse but to bluff.

"Carman cares," she said, fire in her voice. "When she has you, she will reward me with what I need."

"Magic?" I asked. "Not even she has enough to open the doorways. You said it yourself. Do you really want to keep sucking the life from hawthorns like a parasite the rest of your life? Because that's the only reward you're getting if you hand me over."

"Lies!" she cried, her ethereal voice tearing at my psyche. A branch burst from her back, growing and twisting over her shoulder. "You don't even know what you've done, and you call me a parasite?"

"Then end it if I'm such a stain on your kind," I said aggressively. "*End it.*"

She wailed her anger at me, the force burning into my mind, and she struck. The branch streaked toward me, the tip aimed directly between my eyes...

Then...light burst through my vision, and a cry of pain caused me to gasp, but it wasn't my own agony. The branch fell to the ground between us, and Hannah's head whipped to the side.

"*Witch,*" she said, snarling.

CHAPTER 14

"Let him go," a familiar voice commanded.

My head snapped up, and my gaze collided with Aileen. She stood on the opposite side of the clearing, her expression full of anger I'd never seen in her before. And she'd been angry with me plenty of times since I turned up in Derrydun. Those times, I'd shaken in my boots, but this time... She was pure fire.

"A witch and a shapeshifter," Hannah said gleefully. "What a prize."

"Boone isn't yours to win." Aileen snarled and thrust her hands forward.

The branches pinning me in place severed with a crack, and I fell, hitting the ground face first. Splinters turned into ash, and my wounds began to bleed unchecked as I lay there. As I attempted to push myself up, agony seared up and down my broken arms. It was useless. My bones weren't healing fast enough...

"You'll pay for that!" Hannah screeched, her unearthly voice full of a mixture of anger and pain.

She thrust her branches toward Aileen, five more growing from her back, and a high-pitched scream filled the air.

Aileen's hands whipped back and forth like she was dancing, bursts of light slicing through the air. Her magic cut through the approaching branches like blades, cutting down Hannah's attack easily.

More branches replaced the fallen, then more and more until there were too many for Aileen to cut through. They surrounded the witch, twisting and tangling, pinning her arms against her sides and locking her ankles together.

"You're trapped," the fae said triumphantly. "Where to now, Aileen? Would you like to pay a visit to Carman's well of magic? Or maybe you would like mine better. Your power could feed me for a hundred years...*Crescent.*"

"Like hell," Aileen said, her voice dripping with hostility.

"You have no choice. This is the end of the Crescents. *Finally*...and to think it was me who caught you. *Me!*"

I glanced wildly between the pair. But it wasn't

the end. Aileen's daughter Skye... She'd been hidden all these years...

While the fae was basking in her own cleverness, Aileen wriggled her hands free, working her arms against the roots that bound her. Then with a quick burst of magic, she was free before Hannah realized what was happening.

"If I'm going down, then you're coming with me," Aileen cried, slamming her palms down on Hannah's face. "Eat Crescent magic, *you bitch!*"

Searing heat exploded from the witch, and I shielded my eyes as the burst of light hit me.

Hannah wailed as Aileen's power collided with her, the sound reverberating through my bones. The luster of her branches began to turn gray, the life bleeding from her leaves as they broke away from her stems and fluttered to the ground. The echo of her agony made my head throb, her screams endless.

Golden light poured from Aileen's hands as branches and roots circled around the pair in a whirlwind of flying leaves, and it was then I realized the ground was opening beneath them.

"Aileen!" I cried, dragging myself across the earth. My elbows dug into the ground, the wounds on my arms and legs stinging as I closed the gap. *"Aileen!"*

Crescent magic twisted and turned, whipping up

a frenzy in the middle of the clearing as she fought the onslaught from the fae. Dirt, leaves, and debris flew around and around like a tornado, stinging my exposed skin. Every time I attempted to drag myself forward, I was pushed back.

Forcing my magic to flare, I attempted to change my shape. I could be a fox, a gyrfalcon, a black stallion, anything at all to be able to leap to Aileen's aid, but whatever Hannah had done to my mind stopped me from changing forms.

My arms and legs were broken, and although I could feel them knitting back together, they still hindered my own magic from taking hold. I was completely helpless.

Aileen cried out, forcing her magic to flare hotter, and the ground heaved beneath them. Then they began to sink. Down, down...until they were up to their waists in the churning quicksand Aileen's spell had created.

The pressure was too much for Hannah to withstand, and the fae disappeared below the surface, her limbs and branches turning gray. The wind ceased, and for an unnatural moment, debris hung in the air, suspended by the remaining charge of the magical battle, then fell back to earth.

Aileen jerked, her head flopping forward. The ground bubbled beneath her, the dying roots tightening their grasp on her body. She was being dragged under inch by inch, the earth swallowing her whole along with what remained of the fae who'd tricked us all.

"Aileen!" I cried, dragging myself toward her. Pain burned through my arms, but I ignored it, desperate to get to the witch before she was pulled under entirely.

"Boone, keep your distance," she said, holding up her hand.

All I could see was The Tower with its storm clouds and crumbling facade. *The Tower must fall in order to be rebuilt.* Aileen had been drawing it for months, which could only mean...

I pushed up onto my knees, a hairsbreadth away from the churned up quicksand. "You knew this was going to happen, didn't you?"

"Listen to me," she said. "We don't have much time, and there is much I need to tell you."

"Aileen," I wailed, grasping her hand. "You can't leave me. I'm sorry. *I'm sorry!*"

"It's not your fault, Boone. They would've found us eventually. *It's not your fault.*" Her grip tightened around mine as the roots snaked around her waist and dragged her deeper. "Now, listen."

I nodded, willing to do whatever it took to redeem myself. *Anything.*

"Your role in this story was always going to be greater than mine," she began. "The Tower..." She cried out as the roots squeezed around her belly. "Skye will come when she hears of my passing. The call of the Crescents is in her blood, and fate will bring her here, no matter her circumstances. She doesn't know who she is, Boone. You must help her. Guide her. Help her magic awaken. She's the last Crescent. *The last.*"

"How? How can I show her what I don't understand?"

"You don't need to understand," she replied, a tear rolling down her cheek. "You can't tell her. She must discover it for herself. Her legacy will guide her, but you... You must protect her, Boone. You know what's at stake."

"Everything," I whispered.

"Find Robert O'Keeffe," she added as her shoulders sank below the earth. "He'll know what to do next."

"Aileen..." I said with a moan. "I don't know how to do this without you..."

"You can do this, Boone," she whispered. "I've seen it... *Promise me.*"

"*I promise.*"

She was dragged under until her chin grazed the earth around her, and the only thing remaining of Hannah was the churning roots that had ensnared Aileen.

"Thank you," I murmured, tears spilling down my cheeks. "For everything."

"Go," she said in a grating voice. "Go back to Derrydun. Protect them... Protect...*her.*"

The earth heaved... Then...

Aileen was gone.

CHAPTER 15

S taring at the closed sign that hung on the inside of the door of Irish Moon, I frowned.

Two weeks had passed since Aileen's death, and I still expected her to be sitting behind the counter with her tarot cards in hand, forcing another reading on me. The witch had been my mentor, but more importantly, she'd been the closest thing to a mother I'd ever had. She'd helped me when I had nothing and when I was lost inside my own mind. That was why her loss was so hard to handle. She had given me life.

It was dark inside the shop. Not even the muted hum of crystal energy cut through the hardened shell that had grown over my heart.

Thinking about the conversation I'd had with Hannah in the clearing, I grimaced. She'd seemed to know who I was and what I'd done, but the secret of my true identity had gone with her to the grave. All I knew was that my past somehow intertwined with Carman and the plight of the witches. I believed that, somehow, I'd fought for something bigger than myself, and I was hunted for it. I was on the side of good, or at least, I hoped I was. There was no way of knowing for sure, but right now, hope was enough.

Aileen... How she'd known to find us, I would never know, but she'd sacrificed herself to save me without a second thought. All this time, she'd been prophesizing her own death, and I'd been the catalyst.

In her last moments, I'd made a promise to help her daughter...the daughter she'd never had the chance to see grow up. How could I look Skye in the face knowing that if not for me, her mother would still be alive, and she would still be safe on the other side of the world?

I didn't know, but I had to.

It wasn't until the next morning had dawned that I realized I'd witnessed true Crescent magic. The purest, ancient witch legacy there was in the whole of Ireland. That was what Skye would inherit, and I had to be there to protect her.

Honestly, all of this chaos... I owed the Crescent Witches everything.

Movement beside me drew my attention, and I glanced down at the man who'd found me lingering on the street. He was rather short, the top of his bald head barely reached my shoulder, and his belly was round, giving him a rather jolly appearance. His suit was ill fitting, but it only added to his friendly character.

"Boone," the man said. "All right?"

I nodded. "As well as I can be, Robert."

"It's strange to see the shop closed," he went on. The strange little lawyer Aileen had asked me to see was full of his own mysteries. "I almost expect her to come and let us in."

"To be sure..."

"Are ye likin' your new accommodation?" he asked. "I trust it suits ye well enough?"

"Aye." I couldn't stay at Aileen's cottage, considering it all belonged to her daughter now. After a few days on Sean McKinnon's couch, Robert had assisted in finding me a small cottage a mile down the road, still well within the boundary of the hawthorns. It was a fixer-upper, but the work had kept my mind busy, though at night...

Thinking of Hannah, I wondered how she managed to deceive us all.

"I don't understand why no one remembers Hannah," I said. "It's as if she was never here at all. It's strange."

"She was one of the higher fae," Robert explained. "Trickery was her nature, Boone."

"I never had an inkling she was more than human. Not once. Do you think Aileen knew?"

The lawyer shrugged. "It was always hard to tell what she knew."

"She never mentioned you, either."

Robert chuckled and patted his belly. "Us wee folk have to look out for ourselves," he said cryptically.

The sound of screeching tires interrupted our conversation, and we glanced up as a silver car careened around the hawthorn in the middle of the road and came to a halt in the coach bay beside Mary's Teahouse.

"Ahh, right on time," Robert declared.

I raised an eyebrow, watching as a woman unfolded her long legs from the car and stood beside it, slamming the door closed. She was tall, her long black hair sweeping halfway down her back. She was quite beautiful to look at, and for a moment, I was stunned.

Her skin was as pale as ivory, and her figure was slender, the curve of her waist slight. She was wearing a short dress, the dark, floral fabric wrapping around her body and fluttering to mid-thigh, and scuffed black combat boots were laced up on her feet. She looked like a grown-up version of Mairead.

Thinking of the MP3 player with its carefully

curated playlist the young girl had given me after Aileen had passed, I smiled to myself. A show of strength always came with a side of softness. Mairead cared for Aileen more than she'd ever let on, but somehow, I was sure the witch knew all along.

Finally catching my breath, I stared at the woman with a burning curiosity I'd been unprepared for. I already knew it was Skye—I could sense something familiar lying dormant inside her —but I turned to Robert for confirmation.

"Is that her?" I asked. "Is that Skye?"

"Aye," the lawyer said. "That's her. The spittin' image of her mam, don't you think?"

She was, but I could also see hints of what must be her father's looks and temperament. The longer I stared at her, the deeper I fell. *Skye.*

How was I meant to protect her when I was so lost myself? I didn't remember who I was, and that could be the most dangerous thing of all. What if Aileen was wrong about me? Doubt after doubt crept into my mind, causing my heart to twist painfully. What if the same thing happened to Skye?

"Aileen wouldn't have asked ye if she didn't believe in ye," Robert said, sensing my uneasiness. "Things are gettin' worse, and Skye might be the only witch who can stop Carman."

"But I can't tell her," I muttered.

"No. I never understood witches and their laws, but it must be done. Skye must discover her magic on her own. Otherwise..."

He didn't finish his thought, but I knew the ending.

"It's a shame it took something like this to understand why Aileen was always so vague with me," I muttered.

"It's all about the journey, Boone," Robert replied. "It's pointless to give ye a map when the destination doesn't matter. How else are ye supposed to learn?"

"The hard way."

He laughed and slapped me on the arm. "I best be on my way or else Skye will fall victim to Mrs. Boyle's broomstick before long."

"Aye, not the warmest welcome," I said, knowing I would get my chance to speak with her at Aileen's funeral.

Robert crossed the street, swaying back and forth like a penguin hopping over an ice field.

I backed away as he raised his hand in a wave, drawing Skye's attention. She turned, and when she saw the lawyer, her face lit up with a smile.

Warmth tickled my skin, and I knew it wasn't a byproduct of the early arrival of the summer sunshine. Glancing back at the hawthorn in the middle of the road, I smiled softly as the leaves fluttered and gently pulled toward her. The trees were welcoming a new witch to the fold.

The Crescent legacy had called Skye to Derrydun just as Aileen said it would. Now it was up to me to watch, wait, and protect.

The survival of magic depended on it.

OTHER BOOKS IN THE CRESCENT WITCH CHRONICLES

series is complete!

The Crescent Witch Chronicles is a series stuffed full of Irish charm, myth, and mayhem. Come on an adventure fraught with danger and romance...and the ultimate battle to save magic before it's gone forever.

Crescent Calling #1
Crescent Prophecy #2
Crescent Legacy #3
Crescent Rogue #4

Find out more at: www.nicolertaylorwrites.com

ABOUT NICOLE

Nicole R. Taylor is an Australian Urban Fantasy author.

She lives in the western suburbs of Melbourne dreaming up nail biting stories featuring sassy witches, duplicitous vampires, hunky shapeshifters, and devious monsters.

She likes chocolate, cat memes, and video games.

When she's not writing, she likes to think of what she's writing next.

Follow Nicole Online:

Website: www.nicolertaylorwrites.com
Facebook: facebook.com/nrtaylorwrites
Newsletter: www.nicolertaylorwrites.com/newsletter
Email: nicole.this.is@gmail.com

Want more novels just like this one? Check out Nicole's other series:

THE ARONDIGHT CODEX - An ancient war with demons. A lost sword with the power to end it all. And a woman with purple hair is the world's only hope.

THE CAMELOT ARCHIVE - Set in the same alternate Arthurian world seen in **The Arondight Codex...** Deadly secrets. Murder and revenge. The end of the world is nye and Camelot is the last bastion of hope.

THE WITCH HUNTER SAGA - Vampires and witches collide in this thrilling Urban Fantasy adventure. You've never met vampires quite like these...

THE CRESCENT WITCH CHRONICLES - Witches, shapeshifters, and ancient myth collide in this colourful Irish flavoured series! Come on an adventure fraught with danger and forbidden romance... and the ultimate battle to save magic before it's gone forever.

THE DARKLAND DRUIDS - A woman with no living relatives travels from Australia to the other side of the world to find out the truth of who she is… only to land in the middle of a prophecy of destruction. Druids, witches, fae, and shapeshifters abound in this thrilling magical adventure!

AND MORE TO COME!

Find out more at: NicoleRTaylorWrites.com

See what titles are FREE at: Nicole's Free Reads